Dedicated to the stories that
slip and slide through my life.

CONTENT NOTES

These content notes are available so readers can inform themselves; some readers may also consider these notes to be spoilers. This book includes references to mental illness, self-harm, overdose, sexual harassment, homophobia and homophobic violence, violence that results in death, and references to residential schools and colonial violence.

CONTENTS

GOD ISN'T HERE TODAY

The note was posted on the door. It was scratched out in ink that faded near the end. You could see the swirling lines where a heavy hand had tried to force more ink out, then gave up in an indented trail that petered off the edge of the page. The note itself was taped up in a tilted line, as if the taper had done so in a hurry and only as a last-second precaution in the unlikely event a person, like myself, bothered to show up at the door.

I gently peeled the note off the white wood, brought the paper up to my face, and rested the tip of my nose against it to study the words of God closer.

The letters were shaky, as if written by a trembling hand. The ERE all blended together in a mess of lines. The Y longer than all the other letters, stretching halfway down the page. I knew there was a branch of science you could take that analyzed writing, could let you know if someone was a serial killer, a mom, a firefighter. But since God is all of these things, I guess the handwriting meant nothing more than what it said: *God isn't here today*.

But the note didn't say anything about tomorrow. That could mean God would be in. Or it could mean God wouldn't. Or maybe God would come back someday, but not in the near future. Or God could have written the note years ago and just never bothered to come back. Or *today* could just really mean the today that found me standing in front of God's door.

The only day I'd ever bothered to go down to God's office.

The only day I'd ever actually needed God.

What did God need to step out for anyway? Couldn't God just create anything they needed? Or did God crave what we all crave—peace and quiet? Were they stressed out from a constant barrage of people with just enough time to catch the #2 bus and head all the way downtown? Maybe God was bored, maybe nobody visited anymore, so they thought they could just fuck off and no one would even notice. Maybe.

But for the first time in my life, I longed to hear the voice of God. That was a line I'd heard once, during a radio drama. One of the characters said they longed to hear the voice of God. I guess you could say I longed for the feeling of longing. But maybe that's just too confusing. Maybe it really just means that I needed help and no one was home.

My best friend John was gone on summer holidays, probably spending the time meticulously writing down his dreams. He was so intense about them, but they were so gory I never bothered to really listen. And my other best friend Jude was who knows where. I thought I'd seen him from the bus window on my way downtown today, hanging out with the stoner kids who dressed all in black with silver studs and stuff, but he may have been a mirage. It was really hot out.

The point is, I needed help.

So I decided to try the doorknob anyway. Maybe God wasn't all the way out. Maybe they were just sleeping on the couch under a newspaper like my mom does sometimes.

I pushed on the door, and the hinges squeaked as it scraped against the floor. It got stuck about halfway, but I crept in through the opening. My feet caught on something soft and I tripped forward. I caught my balance before I hit the ground.

The room was still, except for a small breeze produced by the whirring of a ceiling fan. Midday light poured in through the large windows. God had a corner office. Small, though. And dusty.

I looked down to see what I'd tripped on and found my feet stood among a mess of letters. Stamped on the front of some were what looked like angry red marks. I picked one up. *Overdue*. It looked like God had forgotten to pay rent. There were tread marks on the envelopes, but it was impossible to tell if God had been stepping on them for months or if it they were from other wanderers like myself.

I walked over to the closest window and looked out. The street below was full of small, vibrant vehicles, the sun reflecting off their metal surfaces in blinks as they moved through the spaces between green and red lights. Sweat was starting to build on my upper lip and hairline. Even with the fan, the room was hot. I gripped the hot metal of the window's edge and pulled. The window came undone with a thwack, then proceeded to screech as I pulled it open enough for the sound of soft honking to filter in. The breeze helped with the stuffy smell of dust, books, and—I peeked into the wastebasket—an old sandwich, left to grow a thick layer of green mould.

I was curious to see what God read, so I wandered over to the sagging bookcase. Lining the shelves were important-looking titles in languages I didn't know. I pulled one off the shelf and opened it—and out fell an old Archie comic that must have been wedged between the pages. I put the boring book down on the shelf and picked up the well-worn comic off the floor instead. The paper was soft with hundreds of turnings.

I looked around and saw that the only truly comfortable place to read, or wait for God, was the threadbare brown couch set against the farthest wall. Above it was a series of photographs depicting the harsh light of the desert, mountains of sand sifting themselves in the wind. Reforming. That, I guess, was a kinda good way to think about God. But

I think a real painting would have been nicer. Presumably, God knew all the greatest painters. They could have asked to borrow some art.

I dropped my backpack down on the ground beside the couch and sat. The seat sagged a little, but otherwise it was a really comfortable couch. Like really, really comfortable. The back shifted to conform to my shape and the material was old but breathable. I leaned in and took a sniff. A faint scent of lavender.

I flipped through the pages and tried not to look at my watch. I knew my dad would be finishing work soon in his woodshop and would want my help around the house. He always helped. He hated when I was idle. My mom would be outside, tanning herself brown in this heat, probably all day on a good sun day like today. But me, I just needed God to show up so I could ask them a question.

I was starting to rehearse my question when I heard a timid knock on the partially open door. I realized I'd for-gotten to tape the note back up—instead I had shoved it into my front pocket. I stayed completely still. Maybe they would just go away.

They knocked again. And again. And then the door started to move.

I decided I had to do something. There was a big desk in the corner, big enough for me to hide under. I put down the comic and was about to flee to the desk when a face peered around the door frame.

"Hello?" The word, hushed, with a note of reverence, came out of the mouth of a small woman. Deep wrinkles ran from the side of her mouth into her greying hairline. "God?" she whispered when she saw me.

I could feel heat in my cheeks. "No." I looked around the room. "I mean, I'm like you."

She put her weight behind a last shove at the door. It opened all the way as she pushed into the room.

"I've been waiting for you," she whispered, shuffling toward me.

"I'm not who you're looking for, I'm not them."

"I just need to ask you for one thing."

"I can't help you." I was exasperated.

"You must." With a groan, she dropped into the chair in front of the desk.

I stood awkwardly between the couch and the desk. My backpack was on the floor beside the couch. I started to inch toward it.

She began to cry. Not a wail or anything, more like a small leaking of tears. Her bony shoulders shook, not a lot, but enough that I stopped.

I looked at the door. The hallway on the other side was dark and empty, I needed to get out of the room and away from her.

I looked at the woman in the chair. She was so small. She reminded me of my grandma, dead two years. And then I thought if my grandma was in this room, waiting for God, and there was another person in this room too, I would want that person to wait with her. So I walked to the desk and sat behind it. I could at least stay till God showed up, or until the woman had to leave, or until someone else came.

I didn't quite know what to do, so I pushed forward a box of Kleenex. It looked full, at least. She took one with trembling fingers and continued to weep. I was embarrassed by how bad I was with emotions, so instead of looking at her I looked out the large window, past the smudges on the glass, into the sky. It was one of those perfect deep blue skies with white edges, a cloudless summer day that always seems to happen on days when I have to be inside.

I wiped my forehead on the sleeve of my T-shirt in an awkward movement. But the lady didn't seem to notice. She was staring down at her fingers, twisting the Kleenex between them.

"I should have come earlier, I know," she whispered.

"You don't have to say anything," I whispered back, hoping she would stop talking so we could just wait in silence.

"I should have come earlier, I should have said I was sorry then, instead of waiting till now, until I was an old woman, until everyone was dead and gone and left me alone."

My feet twitched as my eyes flicked from the doorway to my backpack. I picked up a pen and nervously started to flick the end of it. The woman looked up, and in her blurry eyes, I saw something flash. Anger. Or maybe annoyance. I put the pen down.

"I'm sure they forgave you," I said. I didn't know what else to say. This woman was older than me by tens of years stacked on top of each other. There was nothing I could say that she didn't already know.

"They never did."

"How do you know?"

"I saw it in their eyes. Both of them. They never forgave. They never forgot."

"What happened?" I blurted out the words.

She looked down at her fingers again. "I killed their baby."

I gasped. "You what?"

"I don't remember everything. Not wholly, at least. Or maybe I only remember what I want to remember. Time can be so messy when you're looking at it in a straight line. But the result is the same." She looked up from the desk and into my eyes, as if challenging me. "I killed my sister's baby."

"How?" I whispered into the silence between us.

A bit fat tear hung suspended off her chin. "I drowned it."

My skin prickled. "On purpose?"

"I don't think so."

What could I do?

I pushed the chair back from the desk, all set to rise and leave—to grab my bag, forget about God, forget about my question, forget about the bus ride, the sun, the mouldy sandwich, and just go home.

But she grabbed my hand, faster than I would have imagined possible for someone her age. She reached out, gripped it. Hurt it even.

"You have to forgive me. Or burn me. Or something. You need to end it. I'm begging you."

And she was. I could see it in her eyes.

But I wasn't God.

"I can't do anything for you."

She dropped back deflated, her hand releasing mine. Her voice was weak again, soft. "Why not?"

I stood up. The chair swivelled behind me and hit the wall.

She stood then too, came toward me, and fell at my feet. "You have to." She gripped my jeans. Held the fraying knees. Looked down at my red Converse sneakers. "You have to."

I reached down to try to loosen her fingers from around my knees. Her presence was suffocating—I could feel my lunch rising in my throat, threatening to coat us both in undigested Cheetos and bile. "No one can forgive you," I said, "Only you can forgive you, or it won't count."

That was true, I guess.

She let go then. I couldn't get around her body, though, so I crouched down and patted her back, even though I really didn't want to. But it felt like something God might have done. And she was crying at my feet and she was so old and there was nothing I could do for her, so patting her back didn't seem that bad. She felt mushy. And sweaty. But

I kept patting her back. When my legs got sore, I settled into a lumpy, folded mess beside her, one of my legs splayed under the desk, the other tucked beneath me. She kept her face turned away from me. I kept my hand on her slick back, the damp black material of her shirt clinging to my hand.

I spoke into the underside of the desk. "I need an answer too."

My eyes trailed lines of dusty cobwebs. I didn't want to look at her. She didn't move. She just kept breathing into the carpet.

"I don't know what to do." I wiped my forehead on my sleeve again. The room was warmer with the two of us breathing so close. "I don't think my parents are really my parents. I think they stole me."

I glanced over at her. I couldn't tell if she'd even heard me. I untucked my leg in a gangly movement and leaned against the wall, the whole time keeping my sweaty hand on her sweaty back. I didn't want to keep talking, but there was a comfort in being under the desk. And about this lady. About knowing that whatever I said, it would be okay, because she had killed a baby. And I still needed an answer to my question.

God wasn't here, but she was.

"I think I've always had this feeling. Of being apart from them. Of being another. It was little moments, you know. Like them looking at each over my head. Of them falling quiet when I said something. But last week—"

I paused. I could feel her eyes on me, at least one of them peeking out from behind a bent arm.

"Something happened. I was so angry that day. I could feel it inside me from the moment I woke up. It was pulsing anger, and it flared whenever someone tried to speak to me. I knew it was irrational. I knew I should just stay locked in my room, under the blankets, but my parents forced me out of the house. My dad hates it when I'm not doing anything. You gotta work hard to have a good life, you need purpose to have a good life, you need skills to have a good life, on and on, he just never lets up with this good life bullshit. My mom, she just nods along, but I can tell she doesn't really care, she just loves my dad. So they forced me out of the house.

"We went to a market run by a few volunteer groups at this church by my house. We were walking around, looking at the stalls, and I was being pushed by so many people because it was so busy, and I just felt my body vibrating with rage. I was consumed with anger. I couldn't help myself.

"And then this woman appeared, with a high-pitched voice that pierced its way through the crowd and drilled into my brain. She was yelling at a homeless man who was just resting under a tree. He had this bike with a ton of shit strapped on it. And it was attached to a shopping cart that was piled high with junk, but it was clearly his junk. He had it tied down with bungee cords. She was yelling at him to leave, to take his junk and leave, because he was disturbing the peace.

"I flipped. I don't know what really happened, but I pushed my way through the crowd and I just started screaming at her. I wasn't even fully speaking English, I don't think, it sounded like another language. I started to grab the tent poles surrounding her booth. I was just so angry because here she was, this woman, at an event with good volunteers and church-loving people, and she was yelling at a homeless dude with everything he owned literally strapped to this cart, yelling at him to leave because he was ruining their shitty, loud, crowded event. It was so hypocritical. I started to rage through all the other booths too because fuck them. They were all fake good people.

"And there was a moment, when I was in the middle of that rage, when I saw my parents out of the corner of my eye. They were looking at me like they didn't know me. Like they didn't want to know me. And I heard, I swear I did, even through the chaos, I heard my dad say to my mom, 'Well he's not my kid, that's for darn sure.' My mom clung to his sleeve and I could see her crying, but she never said anything back.

"I ran away after that, just for a night, but they never came looking for me. When I came back in the morning they were sitting on the back patio. They looked surprised to see me."

The woman was sitting up now. Her breathing had calmed down and she was holding my hand. "That doesn't mean they're not your parents. All parents are shitty, even when they don't want to be. All people are, really, when you get down to it."

"Maybe."

"Well." She let go of my hand and hauled herself up off the floor. "I'm going to go now. I'll be back tomorrow. Are you going to be in?"

"Maybe."

She sighed before disappearing into the hallway.

I sat there for a while, staring into the space under the desk, until the sky had turned dark and the only light in the office came from the street lamps outside. I thought about what she'd said, and how maybe that was enough. Maybe I didn't actually need to hear from God for this one.

I stood up, replaced the chair into its position behind the desk. Replaced the pen where I'd found it. I slipped the comic back into the book and replaced it on the shelf, not wanting God to have to search for it when they came back.

Once I was in the hallway, I closed the door behind me, then slipped my hand into my front pocket. The note was crumpled and a bit damp, and the ink had smudged a little, but you could still read the message. I wedged it into the door frame, the letters still legible. *God isn't here today.*

TAKING SPACE

All their clamouring voices, all the spindly hands with decomposing food under their fingernails, who grip at my robe demanding a place beside all the other fine voices.

They drown out the reliable voice I've come to trust inside my own head.

All their voices interrupt my afternoon naps, will themselves to the forefront of my hearing. Spill their decrepit secrets into my ears until I can't stand it anymore.

All their clamouring voices desecrate my soul with the filth they carry that transfers to me with every word I write.

All their clamouring voices pull me under.

All their clamouring voices drive me insane.

All their clamouring voices fill me to empty.

ASLEEP TILL YOU'RE AWAKE

I went to the walk-in clinic because I'd started falling asleep in weird places.

The first time happened in a grocery store. I was holding two boxes of cereal and I got tired, so I sat down in the aisle. I'd never thought to just sit down in a grocery store, but when your eyes are burning and the blinks come slower and slower, it becomes impossible not to. So I sat. And then I leaned. I should never have leaned. I should have sat up straight, like someone who does yoga, but I don't do yoga. I don't even stretch, really.

So I sat, then leaned, and then a man with a brown coat and black sneakers started shaking my shoulder, asking me if I was dead. Okay, he was asking if I was fine, but basically that's the same thing. So he asked me if I was fine and I said no. And then he just walked away. Like, who does that? I said no, you're supposed to help, but he walked away. I got up. I didn't even buy any cereal. I just went home.

My days kept on like that. Being shaken awake by strangers with glasses, or lumpy sweaters, or stinky breath, or frizzy hair, or dry patches of skin. It was annoying.

I went to a doctor. I sat in the waiting room for, like, forever, and then I sat in the doctor's office for another forever, and then she was shaking my shoulder, the doctor, waking me up. I mumbled an apology that I didn't mean. How many of those do you think we give in a year—apologies we don't mean? I must do a hundred. Or maybe more, maybe more than three hundred even. I don't know. I could track it like a food diary addict tracks calories. But I know I won't.

This doctor, she was in my face and asking me questions—like, I just woke up, lady, give me a second. But you know how it is in those clinics, staff are like little rats, scurrying from one beige office to the next, five minutes staring into the desperate eyes of a person wanting to feel better from a cold, and knowing there's nothing they can do. Like, have you never seen a bus ad before? Fluids and rest, stupid. But no, rich people don't take the bus. They never see the ads us poor people do.

Oh, I should mention that I didn't go to the walk-in clinic by my house. No, I went into the neighbourhood with houses that were all one home each, not ones that were sectioned off into many different apartments and suites like mine, overflowing with kids learning to play the trumpet and clothing strung out on balconies. I'd decided that for this sleeping thing, I needed a real big-shot doctor. But guess what? This doctor had the same dead-eyed look as the ones near my house. Like they were staring at you and thinking about roasting a chicken for dinner.

Anyway, she told me that it was probably nothing, that I was overreacting, but she would order a blood test anyway because it couldn't hurt. And I assumed she only offered that because maybe she made extra money if she sent people to get blood drawn, that maybe she only got paid if she did something other than say two sentences in this small office with its one window and hard bed covered in tissue paper. But I don't know. I never went to the blood-drawing place. I don't like needles.

When I came out of the doctor's office, I saw her.

My mom.

No, I should say, my dead mom.

She was sitting in a chair reading a magazine. A boring magazine too. One she would never have read when she was alive—about gardening, or, at least, it had a flower on the cover. But anyway, she was reading it, and she had her legs crossed just like I remember her always sitting, one foot caught behind her calf, her big toe keeping everything in place. Her hair was the same as always, a short burgundy-dyed bob cut on an angle up her jaw.

The tiny hairs on my neck stood up. I was seeing a ghost and no one cared. No one even moved. I started to laugh. It was this belly laugh kind of thing. It spewed out of me, all over the waiting room. But she didn't even look up. My dead mom. She just kept reading her magazine about rotting plants and bugs that trample all over yardwork. And I kept laughing through the cracks in my teeth.

She was wearing the same sandals and shorts she wore the day she walked away from me for the last time. We were in another place then, a town, a dusty kind of beat-up-houses-and-scraggly-brown-grass-with-garbage-just-thrown-out-of-windows-and-dogs-roaming-free kind of place. My dead mom lived there with her fiancé, what's his name. I went to visit because I needed to leave the sounds of the city digging into my brain.

I could tell he didn't want me there. He'd already claimed my dead mom as his own; he'd even put a tarnished brass ring on her finger. The skin under it was this sickly green that leached into her. So that even her once-blue eyes turned from clear ocean water to muddy, stagnant, moss-covered pond. He was like an infection that can't be treated with antibiotics, sores oozing white pus.

I stayed because I knew he wanted me gone.

But I couldn't not fight with him. Or her, by the end. I don't even know why. I just couldn't hold the words in. I tried. Really, I did, but when someone is just so wrong about everything, you have to say something, right? And when not saying something makes you clench your teeth so hard and for so long that the front ones start to wiggle free and are in constant pain, so much so that you can only consume liquid dinners, well, you have to let the words burst free. So I did. And then my mom started to hate me. I think. But I don't really know.

They took me to the bus stop, dropped me off like an unwanted couch infested with moths. But I couldn't stop saying things. So we yelled at each other until we were hoarse, and when she walked away from me I tried to yell that I still loved her even though she'd fallen in love with a human pile of garbage. But she didn't hear me because of all of the yelling from before. She didn't even turn around for one final look.

Her neighbour told me on the phone one day last month that she was dead. And I could only think of how if he hadn't been an open sore leaking congealed waste, she would have heard me when I said I loved her. But instead, on our final day, I saw her back as she walked away, her shorts and sandals, her bob cut too jagged around her neck, yellow shirt with a stain over the left hip.

I decided to sit in the chair beside my dead mom, even though I was finished with the beige room and the not-caring doctor, and I had to go home to let my cat out of the bathroom where I kept her when I left the house so she didn't pee on my mattress again. I sat right beside my dead mom and waited for her to notice me. I breathed her in. She smelled like this gross lavender perfume. Who wants to smell like a dead plant-baby? That's what flowers are, in a way, dead plant babies that hang off stems. She had it slathered on her skin and behind her ears and on her wrists, and I breathed it in deep and realized my mom had never smelled like anything other than garlicky BO when she was alive. Maybe in death you get to choose your smell from the expensive perfume aisle.

I looked at her finger. The green sickness was gone, her skin was bare. She had left the human garbage man. She was finally free. I wanted to vault into the air and scream in glee, but I sat still instead. I didn't know the rules for ghosts. I was afraid a breeze might blow her over and melt her away. So I leaned back in the chair and waited for her look at me.

A nurse with crinkled skin shook me awake. Her face was right in mine and her hot breath poured into my nostrils. I recoiled.

She was saying something about me needing to leave. They were closing.

I reached for my dead mom, but I was alone in the room with the crinkly nurse.

My heart hammered, like, for real, hammered in my chest. It hurt. Where was my mom? Why hadn't she woken me up before she left?

Why had she walked away?

Why hadn't she turned around?

The next day, I couldn't stop thinking of her sitting in the doctor's office. I'd found her, but I had let myself fall asleep. I was stupid. And dumb. An idiot. I should have reached out to her. I should have whispered into her ear. I should have said I was sorry. But I didn't.

The thoughts were burrowing by then. They'd nested in my frontal cortex and now they were burrowing and taking over all the other pathways of my brain.

I couldn't stop myself from going back. I headed straight to the doctor's office. She had to be there, right? What would you have done? Just not gone back? When you knew there was a chance your dead mom would be sitting in a chair waiting for you?

But she wasn't there. Not the next day either. Or the next. Or the next. Or the next infinity of days.

I sit in her chair now when I wait for her. The one she was in when I saw her. And I still smell the lavender perfume. Not, like, a lot. But a little. A whiff. Like when you're sitting outside in the summer and the breeze carries a hint of rotting garbage and you want to get up and go inside, but it's just so nice in the sun, so you try to smell past it. When I sit here I imagine following her back to where she came from. There must have been a portal nearby, or maybe a gateway to heaven or maybe hell. Or maybe, when my mom died, she went to live with aliens. She always liked talking about aliens. Reading about them too. And watching YouTube videos filled with men yelling about how aliens were coming to get us. But I don't really know about that. Why would aliens be interested in a garbage planet filled with garbage people? I guess maybe they'd come for the penguins. I would travel the universe to watch penguins slide around, wouldn't you?

I try not to fall asleep when I sit here waiting for her. I keep my eyes as wide as possible so I don't miss the moment of arrival. Because this time, I'm going to say something. I'm going to say sorry. I'm going to really tell her I love her. I'm going to ask her to take me with her this time. To live with the aliens. Or in heaven. Or even hell. I don't care.

MICKEY'S BAR

MICKEY

The faded navy-blue sign that hung above the entrance was bloated with water damage, but everyone in Lily's Lake knew the place was called Mickey's Bar.

When you stepped inside, the first thing you noticed was the smell. Like a hybrid lemon-lavender tree had planted itself into the deep dark corner and bloomed every night.

After the smell, you might notice the lack of dust—the grime that would normally mark a dive bar. The place was scrubbed clean and looked well-cared for, though the furniture was old and scratched up, repairs done by a semi-competent hand.

The music on the jukebox was classic country, Johnny Cash and Willie Nelson scratching out harmonies—unless anyone had a spare quarter, and then it'd spill out music by the decade. The drinks were simple, and everything on the menu was cooked in one deep fryer: beige with a side of ketchup. You could drink water from the tap and just hang, or sit quietly pickling your liver at the bar. No one much cared what you did, least of all the owner.

Mickey Pelemy was exactly who you'd expect to own a bar called Mickey's Bar. The sort of guy who lived in a small one-bedroom apartment above it, who only saw the sun through its windows. Mickey was the type of guy who'd watch you quietly as you gave him your order without needing to know anything about you. He was the sort of person your eyes ran over, taking in only the big details: how he wore only black T-shirts and dark blue jeans, how he'd only smile a half-grin, and only when he didn't know people were looking at him.

Mickey had spent his life shuffling his heavy feet behind the bar. He knew every bump in the counter's wood, every dent in the linoleum. He knew the flickering pattern of every light and when they were about to blow. He knew how to stack the glass bottles of liquor in front of the cloudy mirror so they didn't topple. He knew how many people could be inside the bar talking and laughing before he had to adjust the music level. He knew that on Fridays, the boys playing pool in the corner needed a pitcher every half-hour. He knew the kids, who'd grown up from their first drink to the hard faces lining the stools every night. He was Mickey's Bar.

Mickey stocked the bar on Mondays. The delivery van would pull up and he and the driver would carry the boxes into the small alcove behind the back door. They always shook hands before the driver climbed back into the cab and drove away. And Mickey always took a second, before opening the back door and hauling the boxes into the store room, to let the sun warm his face, to heat the blackness of his T-shirt, so he could carry the sun with him all day inside the dark bar.

When he was alone, he smiled differently. It was a smile that came from his insides. It gripped his face and spread it wide. Mickey knew this smile was scary, so he never showed it in public, but when he was alone, with the sun in the alley behind his bar, Mickey would smile his face-spreading smile.

✦

As Mickey carried the last box into the back room, the door slammed behind him, letting in a small breeze. His arms strained with the weight.

He noticed the drip drip drip of the pipe overhead was at it again. Brown water had sprawled over the beige linoleum floor in a mess.

Mickey sighed into the shoulder of his T-shirt as he wiped the sweat off his face. He stepped forward and lost his balance. The box was too heavy, and it pulled him backward. He let go and tried to catch himself, only to slam the back of his head against the floor.

Pain. He swore. Mickey tried to sit up but couldn't.

His heartbeat hurt in his chest.

His breath whooshed in and out too fast.

A curtain of black drew across his eyes.

⟋

The sloshing brown water tickled his ears as it lapped against his lobes. Mickey groaned and tried to open his eyes. The light overhead hurt, so he squinted. It was cold on the floor. His skin was goose pimpled. He tried to lift a hand to wipe his face but found he couldn't move more than a couple inches out of the water.

His body was too heavy.

He felt the gentle rocking of the water, the floating haze, that summer afternoon feeling of drifting on your back in a lazy stream, watching the grass on the bank. Mickey had never floated in a stream before, but he'd read about it and he just knew this was what those writers were talking about. Feeling content. The sounds of the world muffled, just you and your breathing and the water.

Mickey lay in the brown pool of growing water, enjoying the contented way his body dragged heavy over rocks and dirt, until he closed his eyes, and everything went dark again.

⟋

Mickey was shivering. He cracked an eye.

Music from the bar filtered through the wooden door. He took a deep breath and decided he needed to stand up, or at least sit up, because it was cold and he was finished floating. But his body was still too heavy, so instead he tried to move his head. When he did, a bit, a stabbing pain rocketed through him. His stomach convulsed. Warm bile filled his throat, forcing him to turn his head all the way to the side as yellow liquid dribbled out of the side of his mouth. It was warm on his cheek. He felt a chunk slide by his nose and plop into the water.

It was only then that he noticed the brown water wasn't just brown anymore. It was tinged red too. The back of his head throbbed. He remembered reading somewhere that head wounds bleed more than any other type of wound.

The drip drip drip from the ceiling added more brown water. The pool lapped against the bottoms of the yellow stained walls.

His eyes swivelled around the room. A clump of dirt, hair, and bits of paper were just starting to float in one corner. The fluorescent light above his head swung back and forth as the air conditioner clicked on, and then off. He felt a flood of hatred for that light. How it always bathed him in shadows and never made him look good. How whenever he stood under that light—even if he'd showered, shaved, put on cologne and a green-and-black-patterned shirt—all he could see was the bags like sacs of water under his eyes, the spiked hair at the back of his neck he couldn't reach to shave, the way his stomach just poured over his leather belt, the hunch in his shoulders he could never get rid of.

That fucking light.

Mickey stared into it, and the deeper he stared, the more he felt like he was floating again.

✦

Mickey woke up fuzzy. A small woman with brown hair and a yellow dress was sifting through the pockets of his jeans, which were slung over a pale green chair. He watched her through a slitted eye. She looked like a daffodil. He thought about how long it had been since he'd seen a real-life flower, not just the plastic red ones he put up in the bar at Christmas, which always ended up dusty. She pulled his worn leather wallet out from his back pocket.

What was she doing? He tried to open his mouth, to ask her to please leave his things alone. To please give him a sip of water.

But Mickey couldn't say anything. His words were stuck in his throat. Something rubber was blocking them. A tube. He tried to swallow and gagged a little.

The yellow-dress woman didn't notice—she was too busy opening his wallet and slowly flipping through it. He knew it was mostly empty except for a few bills, a credit card, debit card, and his ID. She pulled that out and flipped it over. There was a small sticker, almost all rubbed off, that read *Organ Donor*. He knew it was there because he'd put it there himself.

She slipped the jeans back over the chair they'd been resting on and picked a clipboard up from the seat. Mickey watched her pen fly over the clipboard, marking things down—about him, he assumed, about who he was.

Before she left the room, she took a step toward the bed, and he felt her hand on his arm. Her fingers were warm, hot even, against his cold skin. He wanted to reach out his own hand and touch her burning fingers, but he still couldn't move. He couldn't figure out why.

Her warmth left him, and he watched her go, her eyes round and open and sad. And then Mickey was alone.

✦

When Mickey came to again, he was only partially aware of the pain. It was like a twisting cramp in his side—no, more like the burn when you walk on a blister, or maybe the feeling you get when you're punched and the wind is knocked out of you and you can't catch your breath. Or a migraine, one that hits you like a knife to the brain. Or the feeling when you see someone you love loving someone else and your heart drops a beat. Or when you double over because of a sharp, incessant pinch—no, not a pinch, a throb—and all you can do is point to your middle.

Mickey felt all those pains at once. But he couldn't see anything, at least not at first. Then he began to see little bits of things. Water rushing over rocks coated in ice. Tall golden grass. A glass filled with whisky. Red blinds. A tarnished key on a black string.

A shiver started to run through him, like he was on a motorbike, like its power was zipping through him. He began to hear what sounded faintly like a TV audience, far away but laughing hysterically. He felt a mouth against his ear, undistinguishable words whispered in a breath that made him tremble. Soft sobbing.

And then Mickey saw something like light.

LUNGS

The back door slammed closed as Tommy ran beside the house toward the front yard.

His ma's wail trailed after him: "Keep off that thing, Tommy."

He spun and grinned at her through a window before hitting the pavement out front. When he reached the street, he slowed to a walk, then pulled a rolled cigarette out of his front pocket. He put it to his lips but didn't light it. He just liked the memory of the feeling.

The block he lived on was one of cement and wires. Long yellow grass between pinched cracks and puffed dandelion heads. It was quiet in the midafternoon with all the kids at school. Tommy felt freer when the sun was in this position in the sky. When everything slowed down.

He'd been out of the hospital for eight months. The key to his bike had burned a hole in his mind—it was his good luck charm. He'd worn it on a frayed black string on his wrist, something to turn over in his fingers as the doctors talked about him like he was already dead.

Tommy pulled the key off his wrist and threw it up in the air, catching it before it hit the ground. He hadn't ridden her since before last summer—he'd been waiting for a day that felt like today. Unpredictable. A day that hung in the air like lightning. When he'd woken up that morning, he'd felt a tightening in his new lungs, like they were taking up too much space in his chest.

He rounded the corner of the block and saw the bike sitting under its tarp in his uncle's driveway. He didn't park it at home because he knew his mom hated it. She'd done so much for him when he was in the hospital, it felt only proper to keep it away from her.

He pulled at the light blue material until it bunched on the ground around the tires. She looked like she always had: shiny, black, gleaming silver. He crouched down and ran a hand over the seat, and a twinge of pain settled into his left lung. Tommy took a deep breath to calm himself. He wasn't going to let his body betray him anymore. He was going to make his life now. He touched the place on his chest where the surgical scars ran in horizontal lines, put his hands right over where the new lungs sat in his chest, and he grinned.

It was Tommy's world now.

He jumped back up and looked around. For a moment everything looked fuzzy—out of focus. The light warbled, the bright sun dimmed, its heat dissipated.

The pain he was so used to feeling was gone, replaced by need. He reached out in his mind and heart for...meaning. He needed a reason. For the first time in his life he needed to understand his emotions, what they meant.

Tommy shook his head in disgust. Meaning hadn't done anything for him before. What he actually needed was to get going, because going was better than standing still, just like living was better than dying. All he had to do was get moving and everything would be like it was before.

Tommy whistled as he puttered around the bike for a few more minutes, making sure everything was how it was supposed to be. When he was satisfied, he jumped onto the seat and inserted the key. The engine roared to life. Tommy grinned as the familiar feeling of power vibrated through him. He wanted to go and he wanted to go fast. No time for thinking. No time for stopping.

But before he could take off, he was overtaken by an intense craving for a ripe lemon, could practically feel its sourness on his tongue. He laughed out loud. Who eats lemons?

And then he was off, gone, and moving toward a future that was as endless as the ocean he lived beside.

SKIN

Grace leaned against the railing. The cold of the metal soothed her hands. She watched the water rushing below her as it fought with the snarled branches for a clear path through the cracked ice, slopping up the muddy banks of the Assiniboine River as it sought the fork where it would join with the Red River.

She looked down at the fiery red hands clutching the metal, saw again their pocked, burned skin. She brought one up and touched her face, where the red skin there had been grafted temporarily with new skin—well, old skin, really. Lived-in skin that had belonged to someone else. Someone dead. Someone she didn't know.

Grace grimaced. The pain she felt all day long thrummed into something more demanding as her curious fingers moved along her right jawline. She gasped into the cold air but continued prodding. The pain made her salivate. She leaned into it and kept going. She wanted to feel what frozen tears felt like. When her cheeks burned both icy and hot, Grace finally let her hand drop. She let out a moan and then a scream.

The ice below her cracked in a boom as it bashed against the banks.

She knew how it felt to have something break off you at every turn. Grace turned from the river.

Red and pink light highlighted the golden tufts of clouds in the distance and the dry brittle grass peeking through the snow. She held her digital camera to her face. Grace needed something to paint tonight and it might as well be this. A sunset fit for her, angry red lines scratching and scarring perfection.

She took a picture. Then she walked away, head down, headed for home. Her backpack, slung over one shoulder, bumped along with her steps. She counted the bumps, one to a hundred, then a hundred more.

Her street was empty, or at least that's how it seemed. So many of the homes in her neighbourhood were boarded-up falling-down garbage piles of unkept should-be-knocked-down-and-burned properties. Grace slipped past the red-and-rusted-with-neglect wire fence that held her family in. The grass that shot out of the dirty footprinted snow betrayed the lack of mowing over many previous summers. Three battered cars, which her grandfather had convinced himself and his wife that he'd fix up were embedded in the dirt around the side of the house. Grace grimaced when she noticed the new Christmas decorations her gran had put up. Plastic elves with mispainted eyes, window clings of blurry snowflakes.

She put her hand on the back door, tried to sense if anyone was around. She cracked open the door and breathed in a tight gasp. The air that came out was steaming hot, the furnace working on high. Grace didn't hear anything, so she opened the door a bit more, and then some more. She peeked around and took in the deserted kitchen, plastic bags piled on the table among the lunchtime dishes.

She heard her grandfather's huff of a laugh coming from the living room. She knew her gran would be sitting next to him, her hands kneading his swollen legs. Grace needed to not be brought into that, into their forced laughter as they stared at the dim TV screen. Her gran trying not to wince as the sores near her grandfather's ankles started to leak, the smell of the poultice she would lay on them before she wrapped the gauze tight and filled the room with an earthy stink. Her grandfather's diabetes literally pushing through his skin.

Grace wanted silence. Cold air. Her bed. Blankets.

She closed the door softly behind her, flipping the lock with a silent click. She debated pausing in the kitchen for something to eat, but then she heard her gran pulling herself up with a grunt and a huff, and scurried instead down the basement stairs.

Grace stood in the dark, her back against the wall, waiting to see if she'd been heard. When the stairway light didn't click on, she exhaled and walked the narrow path through her gran's boxes to her room.

She closed the door behind her, flicked on the lamp beside her bed, and set her backpack on the floor. The window creaked as she slid it open, letting in the frosty air, and for a second she smelled lemons, fresh and strong, as if from the moment the knife slices through the thick skin and juice sprays everywhere. When she breathed in that smell, she felt comfort. The burning pain in her body disappeared, and her aloneness was okay because it wasn't lonely to be alone.

But the scent faded, and she was once again standing in the converted basement storage closet that was her bedroom. She threw off her coat and kicked off her boots, then climbed into her bed and grabbed her sketchbook. She flipped through the pages. So many of them covered in angry black pen strokes. So many of them unfinished. So many of them ruined.

Out of the corner of her eye, she saw a black smudge by the wall—but when she tried to focus on it, nothing was there. As soon as her eyes went back to the page, though, it was there again: a shape of a man, maybe. Watching. Flickering in and out. Maybe she was finally losing her mind.

Grace felt a longing then, but she couldn't describe what it was for. Nothing, everything, meaning, choice.

When she looked at the wall next, the smudge was gone.

MICKEY

The boy was crouching beside a black motorcycle. Mickey, who had never been on a motorcycle, nevertheless felt the giddiness flowing from the boy.

The last thing Mickey remembered was light. He thought he should be panicking—he wasn't where he was supposed to be; it was daytime and there were things to do at the bar—but Mickey couldn't summon any panic. Everything he felt was dampened. Even the pain that had been radiating from all parts of him in the hospital was now more of a low hum.

He brought a hand to his face and was shocked to discover that one of his eye sockets was empty—he realized he could only see out of one eye. He looked down at himself. Under the black T-shirt he always wore, he could sense that large patches of skin were missing. He patted his back pocket—his wallet was gone too. Everything felt slightly off. Quieter.

He realized that he didn't know his body, not completely anyway, there was too much missing. That too should have made him panic, but it didn't. What a strange thing it is to discover, he thought to himself, that you can know whether your body is yours or not. Mickey had never thought of his body as a place that he was comfortable in until now, until he was no longer fully there.

He looked around. He didn't recognize where he was. There were low houses painted in bright colours with flat roofs, cold air ripping through the small yards between them. He was used to full green trees, mountains in the distance, the smell of the Pacific Ocean, his apartment above the bar. Here, concrete surrounded him like it had been poured out of the sky, splashed over everything. Grey skies stretched to the horizon. From a documentary he'd once seen on TV, it looked like he was near the Atlantic Ocean. The other side of the country. How'd he get there?

He opened his mouth to ask the boy whether this was the Atlantic Ocean, but nothing happened. No sound. No breath. He tried to tap the boy on the shoulder, but he couldn't move close enough. Mickey felt winded, like he'd been running. His head throbbed with a migraine. He tried again to remember how he'd come to be wherever he was.

The light. That was all he could come back to. The light.

He looked up, trying to find it. He could make out the sun from behind the hazy clouds, but the sunlight was different from the light he was looking for.

The boy stood up, and Mickey felt a surge of excitement, an urge to feel wind on his face and miles behind him. The boy turned and looked at him—well, in his direction, but maybe at him? He saw the boy's face tighten and the grin fade, frown lines stretching across his young face. And then the boy turned away and started to whistle, the sound curving around teeth and whooshing past lips.

Mickey watched him jump on the bike, watched it roar to life. He felt the vibration in his own body, and clutched his arms to his chest. The boy whooped and took off, dust trailing behind him, small pebbles raining on Mickey's shins.

Mickey watched him go. As he did, he felt himself become light, and light, and lighter, until he was only white.

HEART

Quinn crouched beside his small fire. He fed it twigs and dry leaves, waiting for it to blaze bright. Once the flame was steady, he stretched out, leaned heavy into his low-slung chair. He cupped the back of his head and stared up.

The moon was high, and the stars held pictures he could never understand. All he saw was a mess of light—not some prophetic code written by gods, not a tapestry of souls held prisoner for eternity, heroes of antiquity held in starlight. Quinn tried to imagine what it would be like to be held in space and starlight. To blaze across the sky for longer than the planet you came from would even exist. To become wiser than everyone who'd ever lived, to be free from anxiety, free from anything that held you prisoner. If you were lucky enough to be pointed in the direction of one you loved, you'd have all anyone would ever need. And if you added up all the people hanging there in the sky, from all cultures around the world and from all of history, well, it would actually be pretty crowded up there, so you'd never be lonely.

But right now, he was alone—and it was daunting to be alone, staring at those who might be staring back, millions of years of wisdom on their side, judging him. So Quinn turned his gaze to the fire in front of him. This firepit was a place in which he could lose himself comfortably. The fire never looked him over and decided he wasn't enough. The fire only kept him company.

Quinn felt the presence of the high Rockies behind him, stretching out in long distant lines of shadows of shadows. He knew them well: their bumpy outlines against the clear blue of the prairie sky, the way they came to him in his dreams, the voices of the Earth checking in to see how he was doing. Quinn had always felt like a member of their stoic pack. He had spent more time with those mountains than anyone else.

He pulled some jerky out his pocket and ripped off a chunk with his teeth. His heart squeezed a few extra beats, and he coughed deeply. That helped sometimes, when his heart stopped its rhythm. Cough deep in your lungs, take an ice-cold shower, shock your system to reset. Reset or die.

Quinn had been living on the border of death longer than anyone else he knew. For his whole life, he seemed to be standing right at the brink, waiting for the final beat of his mangled heart. He rubbed the front of his chest where the scar stretched long and straight—its own kind of constellation written on his skin, one that named him either survivor or dead man walking, depending on your particular view of the world.

Quinn himself truly held only one belief—more like a hope, like that last moment of starlight before the dawn: love. True, deep, real. And not something born of pity, but different and deeper.

He looked through the fire and for a moment he thought he saw a man sitting opposite, a man with an identical scar to Quinn's inexplicably visible through his black T-shirt, but when the flames shifted Quinn saw he was still alone.

He pulled out his phone and found the picture of Mary Ann he'd taken at the last bush party. She was dancing, her arms up in the air, not smiling at him, not even knowing he existed in that moment—he loved the movement in her, the life. Quinn stared into the screen until the bright light burned her image into his eyes. And then when he looked up into the dark sky, he could still see her, up among the ones watching. She danced with them and with him, and hopefully one day they would be destined to dance together in starlight, and it would be for forever.

SKIN

Grace threw the paintbrush in the corner.

Nothing was turning out. The lines were heavy, uneven. The colours mixing into a blah sort of brown. The whole of the canvas was an exercise in futility.

She liked that word. *Futility*. It summed up her whole life.

"Grace," her gran yelled from upstairs.

Grace tried to ignore her, but then her cellphone beeped, more than once. She looked at the screen.

GRACE

UPSTAIRS

FOOD

NOW

Grace sighed into the emptiness of her room. She really didn't want to go upstairs. It would be too hot. The steam of her gran's cooking always made her fresh skin pinch, like it would fall off and leave the raw nerves exposed again. Grace's stomach flipped at the memory of the pain after the accident. She pulled up the hood of her sweater to obscure the sides of her face and stepped out of her cool room.

"Gracie, finally." Her grandpa sat at the crowded table, one foot up on a stool, slurping soup from a plastic bowl with pictures of *Star Wars* characters on it.

Her gran set a steaming bowl of soup in front of Grace, as she slid into the chair closest to the stairs. "Did you book your ticket yet?"

"No, I forgot." Grace tugged at the edges of her hood.

"Well, you don't have to worry, I bought it."

Grace rolled her eyes. "Why?"

"Because you weren't going to and your mom sent the money for the ticket."

"Yeah, right."

"She has a new man," her grandpa said, as he sponged up soup with a thick slice of bannock. "He's rich. You could be too if you went to visit them more. He'd cut you in, I'm sure."

"Wah." Her gran slapped his arm. "Stop it."

"So you mean she picked up some loser and is milking him for his savings before finding some reason to kick him out?"

"Something like that, but, you know, in a classier way."

Her grandpa grinned at her, popping his dentures out and rolling his eyes back, trying to get her to smile. That had stopped working when she was about five, but she still forced out a laugh for him.

"Bus is at seven," her gran said.

"You couldn't get an earlier one?"

"I could cash in the money and make you walk, buy me and the old man a big bucket of KFC, if you'd rather."

"Fine." Grace blew at the soup on her spoon. "Thank you."

She looked up at her gran, who was busy wiping the counters. In the steamed-up window behind her, Grace thought she saw the reflection of a figure: a man in a black T-shirt and dark jeans, his arms folded over his chest as he leaned against the kitchen wall, watching. Grace turned, but the spot was empty. When she looked back at the window, the figure was gone.

"I'm only going for the day," she said to her grandparents. "I'm not staying."

"That's fine. But just try to be nice to her, okay?"

Grace sighed. She always tried to be nice to her mom; it just didn't always work. She breathed in deep and smelled lavender. All the time now, lemons or lavender, following her around. Maybe I'm having a stroke, she thought. Didn't people smell things before that happened?

"Okay, fine, I'll be nice. Whatever that means."

"Thank you, m'girl. Wasn't that easier than fighting?"

Grace smiled down at her soup. She wished she could just make life easier for everyone. But everything was so hard these days. Since the accident.

Her skin burned in a slow pain and she scowled. Fuck. She hated her life.

LUNGS

The curve in the road sharpened to the right. Tommy felt the bike give way before straightening back out. He hunched lower in his seat. The shifting Atlantic Ocean was on his left. It was one of those days when the sun hit it and caused a spray of sparkling light, when the horizon line was indistinguishable from the blue of the water and the blue of the sky. Frosted air seeped past his leather jacket, made him feel alive in a way that not even finding out he was getting new lungs had. The scraggly bushes and trees of the coast were too low to obscure his view, and he pushed the bike faster and faster. It moved with him as he took each curve in a low sweep. He zipped past the tourist villages laid out in long lines of shops by the ocean, lobsters waving on oven mitts, nets nailed to walls for perfect pictures.

He wanted to go somewhere alone, somewhere beautiful. Tommy had never needed to see beauty as much as he had since his surgery. This urge for solitude and beauty had him racing around the island from sunrise to sunset, but he hadn't yet found anything to soothe that raw place inside his chest that clamoured for ultimate beauty. The place where he was stuck back together with the breath memory of the man he held inside of him.

When he couldn't see anything anymore except for blue water and the highway, he veered off to the side of the road and stopped. Turned off the bike and felt its vibration leave his body.

He walked down to the shoreline, stumbling over rocks, slipping down the bank until he hit gravelly sand. The sound of the surf pounded into him. He closed his eyes and felt it churning, foam bubbling in the waves' ferocity. He breathed in the salt, the freezing wind as it whipped his hair around his neck, felt his lungs clench around the air, reject it. A cough gripped his body and he doubled over, spit dribbling out of his mouth as he hung there, spent. Tears watered his face, sliding through the stubble on his cheeks.

When he could, he lowered himself to the sand with a groan, leaned back against the weathered rock behind him. His fingers absently flipped the bike key, the frayed black rope cutting a line across the white skin of his wrist.

His phone rang. Tommy made no move to answer it.

The sun was starting to set—its reflection started to spread across the water, the blue of the sky tinting pink and gold.

The phone stopped ringing, then started again.

Tommy sighed, "Yeah?" He flicked sand off his jeans.

"Where are you?" His brother Mark's voice cut through the solitude.

"Driving."

"You've been gone all day. Again."

Tommy debated hanging up and putting the phone back in his pocket.

Mark continued. "You need to take it easy. Mom is fucking off her rocker. She thinks you got a secret girlfriend, she's been tearing the house apart looking for clues."

"Tell her I'm just thinking."

"About what?"

"I dunno."

"Well just come home, okay?"

Tommy closed his eyes. "I'll be home when I'm home."

"You've been acting—"

"What?"

"Suicidal."

"What the fuck? I just want to be alone—to think, not die. If I wanted to die I would have done it in the hospital."

"Yeah, but—so I looked online, and you're being weird like they say suicidal people are weird. Isolating and shit."

"I just want—" Tommy didn't know how to explain it. He wanted to be content, he wanted quiet, he wanted beauty. And for that, he needed to be alone. "I'll be home soon."

"Fine, I'll tell her."

"Did she go to the library for me? Pick up that book I asked for?"

"What book?"

"Never mind."

"You don't read."

"I can fucking read."

"I know you can, I'm just saying you don't."

"Well, I want to now."

"See, this is what I mean, you're behaving different."

"Later."

Tommy turned his phone off. Was Mark right? Was he suicidal? He didn't think so.

He decided to wait till dark to go home. He always felt faster in the dark anyway and he liked going fast. He pulled a lemon out of the front pocket of his jacket, ripped it in half, and licked the juice as it dripped down his hand. Tommy breathed and marvelled in the simple of beauty of it, breathing.

MICKEY

The boy, Quinn, stood in front of the girl, grinning—a little too much, Mickey thought. She'd never go for a boy who smiled like that. Maniacal.

They stood outside under a night sky, the smoke from the huge bonfires clinging to the tops of the trees that circled the clearing, the sounds of the party dimmer at the edge of clearing where they stood staring at each other.

Quinn fumbled with the drink in his hand, and some of the liquid splashed down the front of his shirt, adding to his dishevelled look. He ran a hand through this hair, which only made it stick out in the wrong places. The thick goo he'd put in it earlier was not helping.

Mickey had watched hundreds of boys try to get a girl's attention. When you own a bar, that's basically your purpose. But there was something about the way Quinn moved that let Mickey know he wasn't just looking to score—he was clearly in love. Mickey could feel it in his own chest, in the empty place where his heart used to sit. He felt it in the way pain pinched him with every beat of Quinn's body.

The pounding of the drums rippled the ground as Mickey walked away from the pair. There's so much just out of reach when you're alive, Mickey thought. He wandered through the milling crowd of people, some dancing, fists pounding the air along with the music, some yelling into ears in the dark, some sneaking off to the tree line for a smoke or a bit of necking. He could still feel Quinn vibrating with excitement and anxiety. The two emotions rolled in a wave over him.

Mickey wished he could leave, go back with Quinn to the mountains, where it was peaceful and quiet. Back to the mountains that stood like sentinels over the valleys. There was something in the way they silently pushed upward—a millimetre at a time, dirt and rock rising from the crust of the Earth—that caused the hair on his arms to rise. They gave him the sense that time was the only immortal thing in the universe. When he sat beside Quinn's fire, Mickey felt the whole world at once, which was a feeling completely different from anything he'd felt at his bar.

Mickey tried not to think about his bar now. The pangs of regret that filled him when he did were overwhelming. But sometimes he wanted to know if his sister had come to look after it, like she always promised she would if something happened to him. Sometimes he wondered if it was even still standing, if anyone even noticed he was gone.

Nothing Mickey did brought him back to the bar. He'd spent quite a bit of time willing himself there. He tried closing his eyes and wishing, but nothing moved him any closer.

Nor had he figured out how he was moving from Tommy, to Quinn, to Grace to... He felt that there were other worlds, just outside his vision, that he hadn't visited yet. Sometimes he could hear snippets of conversations, laughter, sobbing. But he didn't know how to bring them into focus. He didn't know how to do anything anymore, really.

A sharp pain in his chest made him gasp. Quinn. Mickey's vision blurred, and then he was again beside Quinn. Large drops of sweat clustered on the young man's forehead and upper lip. His heart was beating fast, too fast. Mickey clutched his own chest. His breath caught, which was normal these days, but his heart—the hollow place had gone from aching to stabbing.

Quinn stumbled over some words and, in a rush of beer-induced bravery, finally got to the point of this whole evening. "Mary Ann," he started, "I was wondering if you and me, if we could, maybe, go out for dinner or something— but it doesn't have to even be dinner, it could be lunch even, or coffee, or even a walk maybe, I know some great trails, but not like secluded 'I'll murder you' trails."

Lines stretched across the girl's forehead. She raised her eyebrows.

"I just mean, I think you're beautiful."

Before Quinn could continue, two guys came up behind him. The larger one put his arm around Quinn's shoulder and pulled him close into his armpit, where his white tank top was stained yellow. The other guy punched him in the arm.

"Holyyy," the large guy barked with a grin, "I think Quinn here is trying to snag."

The other guy let out a whistle, one that came from the tip of his tongue like a snake. "Quinn, what you think you're doing? You gotta stay in your league, man, you gotta try one of those old girls, the ones with them saggy tits, they're more in your league, man."

Mickey wanted to step forward, tell these punks to scram, but he couldn't move. His chest felt like ice and his limbs were locked into place. Quinn tried to wrestle free of the sweaty man's grip, but the hold was firm.

"Fuck off, Carey," Mary Ann spat at the big guy.

"Well, if fucking is what you want," he said, still grinning.

"In your dreams," Mary Ann said, and she turned and walked away.

"Mary Ann," Quinn hollered at her retreating back.

The other guy patted Quinn's shoulder. "Forget her, dude."

"We're just looking out for you, man," Carey said.

"Yeah, someone with your heart condition, you can't take someone like her, man."

They each shoved their hands in their pockets and sauntered away, soiling the air with their nasal laughter.

Quinn kicked the ground, then crumpled his cup and threw it at them but missed.

Mickey felt his body come alive with a tremble of rage. He reached out a hand, tried to rest it on Quinn's shoulder. He was a good kid. Better than most.

Mickey felt Quinn shiver before he stormed off into the mess of people. But this time Mickey didn't follow. Instead, he moved into the darkness and disappeared.

LIVER

Stephen stumbled to the bar's restroom. He didn't know why they called it that. Restroom. More like a piss room, really.

Once in the piss room, Stephen took a moment to admire his own reflection. A tall, good-looking man, if he ever saw one, looked back at him through the cloudy mirror over the sink. He turned, half-collapsing against the rim of a urinal, and pissed a messy arc in what he hoped was the right direction. Then he wrenched himself back over to the sink and splashed water over his hands. "Gross fucks don't even have the decency to have soap," he muttered. He ended up drying his hands in his curly dark hair, using the water to wipe down the sides, front to back. It gave him an Elvis look, sorta, but not fat Elvis, more like young up-for-anything Elvis. He straightened his black tie and smoothed his grey suit. "You gotta look like a winner to be a winner," he mumbled. Before leaving, he flicked off the light, because the environment was important and Louie the Lightning Bug would be proud.

The mood in the bar had shifted when Stephen stumbled out. He knew it like he knew the rhythm of his own heart. The men in the back were looking shifty, their hands moving too fast, their smiles too quick. The girls were too quiet.

It was time for Stephen to leave.

He bent to grab his heavy winter coat from the stool it was pooled around, but lost his balance and fell into the big guy who'd sat down in the seat next to his. Stephen grabbed the man's leg for support on his way down.

"Hey, faggot, don't go hitting on me."

Even Stephen thought that was a bit much, and he'd called an old woman a fucking tweaked-out bitch that afternoon. "Takes one to know one, don't it," he said with a sly smile. He gripped the edges of his coat, trying to maintain a semblance of being put together.

The man's bar stool flew out from under him as he stood. His hulking figure cast a shadow over Stephen, who was still floundering on the floor. "You should watch your mouth."

"I do all the time, especially around big bears like you."

The guy's hairy fist came down and cracked Stephen's skull. His back molars sliced into the flesh of his tongue.

"That's what I call foreplay," Stephen screamed into the silent bar, his spit flying onto the man's boot. "Do me just like that, sweetie, and I'll be yours all night long."

The man flinched, disgust evident in his eyes.

"Come on," said the bouncer, who had a hold of Stephen and was pushing him toward the door, "you gotta go, man." He whispered into Stephen's ear, "It's for your own good, trust me, people here will rip you apart if you keep acting like this."

"Fuck 'em. What, they can't take a fucking joke?" Stephen began to struggle, the whisky in his blood driving him. "You hear that? Fuck you, you inbred dumb fucks. You can't even take a joke? Like I would even want to fuck any of you hairy assholes."

Another fist came from the left and struck him hard and solid in the side, right above his still weeping surgical scar— he'd just had the stitches out that morning.

Stephen gasped in pain, even as a new sensation hit him: air so cold it stung his skin, burned it, stole his breath.

"Hey, hey," he yelled, "you can't just throw me out here, it's fucking freezing."

When no one answered, he banged on the bar door.

"Give me my fucking coat, you animals. I paid for that fucking coat."

Nothing.

Stephen looked around. His hand held his side. The pain he felt there was radiating outward and mingling with the chill in the rest of his body. His face was already numb from the cold.

He decided to walk to his hotel. It wasn't far. Stephen's breath came out in hot heavy boozy whooshes as he stumbled forward. He'd bought his dress shoes that morning. *With a shine to them*, he'd told the saleslady, *I wanna see myself in my shoes*. She'd handed them to him in sheer boredom, her phone buzzing away in her fist.

It was only a few more blocks to the hotel, a few feet over feet, a few looks up at the stars. The stars, whose light actually penetrated the dim haze covering the small hamlet that passed for—this far north and this close to the mines—civilization. He never saw the stars in the city. In the hospital, the only stars he'd seen were on the TV, waving at cameras over bullshit. Out here, where his breath puffed white, they were clear, crystalline, like he'd always dreamed they would look. They were beautiful.

Stephen decided to take a rest and really look at them, and let himself fall backward into a snowdrift. It was softer than he thought it would be. He nestled back and cupped his neck in his hands. Out of the corner of one eye he saw a faint hint of green in the sky, the start of a dance.

He felt peace in that snowbank. He pulled out his phone and started to scroll through the pictures stored there. His kids' smiling faces stared back at him, younger than they were now, still happy whenever he got around to visiting them. Stephen tapped his contacts, his finger hovering over his son's name. He wanted to call, he should call, but he just couldn't. He knew what the conversation would turn into.

His son would beg him to come home, and Stephen would promise he would right away. His son would beg him to stop drinking, and Stephen would tell him he already had. His son would ask him to be a dad, and Stephen would say he'd try. And then his son would ask why he needed to find work so far away, and Stephen wouldn't know how to tell him that if he didn't find work away from them, he'd feel like he was being locked into a dark closet and suffocated. How do you tell your kid something like that?

Stephen always thought he'd have the time to someday explain his mind and heart to his kids, but time was something he never had enough of. So when the man in the black T-shirt and black jeans, smelling faintly of lavender, sat next to him in the snow, Stephen knew he would finally have all the time in the world—but it still wouldn't be enough to make the call.

MICKEY

The northern lights danced in Stephen's eyes.

Mickey watched him pull a cigarette from his pocket. When his fingers didn't work well enough to flick the lighter, Stephen began laughing instead.

"Figures." He gestured vaguely at Mickey. "You know, I never knew they'd be this beautiful. I figured they'd be like smudges, maybe like a flash of lightning. I never knew." Stephen's smile was soft as his body continued to relax into the snow.

Mickey reclined beside Stephen, the snow holding him but not chilling him. "I used to go up the hill beside my bar on nights like this and watch them dance. Every time felt like the last."

"Where's your bar?"

"Up north. A different north than this."

"Why aren't you on that hill tonight then?"

"I dunno, I can't seem to find it anymore."

"I know what you mean. I can't find home anymore either. I know my kids wish I could but something won't let me. It's like the opposite pole of a magnet. I try to, I buy a ticket, I've tried every way—bus, plane, train—but I just never make it. What's your bar like?"

"It's like a wood table that's been passed down from generation to generation holding every fingerprint, every smudge, every coffee spill and angry word, every touch. Every life that sat at it sits now in its fibre. It's home."

"That must be some bar." Stephen clutched his bleeding side. "I think this might be bad."

Mickey felt the constant ache in his side he'd been feeling since leaving the hospital start to fade.

"You know what I can't get around?" Stephen asked.

Mickey turned his gaze away from the sky to watch Stephen. His face was turning ashy as blood in the snow snaked away from him like a forked river. "What?" he asked.

"I don't think I've ever felt it."

"Felt what?"

"Love. Like the kind you see in movies and read about in books. You know the kind? Even with my kids. I think some people aren't meant for it, you know?"

"I do."

"You strike me as someone who's never felt love either."

Mickey didn't know what to say. The truth was he'd

been in love once. When he was younger. But then she left, and he was alone. Sometimes that's just all there is. One love. One loss.

"I wish I could have one more whisky, you know?" Stephen sighed, and his white breath rose into the sky.

"I never drank."

"You owned a bar!"

"I liked the people, the atmosphere. The memories."

Mickey looked past the northern lights to the clear starry sky. In those stars, he saw his regret. A life lived behind a bar, alone, waiting for someone he once loved to come back, knowing that would never happen. He felt shame. He'd tried to ignore it his whole life, the tiny voice inside that told him he was living wrong, but he'd stayed, he'd never left. He always told himself he would, that he'd go out into the world and stop hiding, make something of his life, but then he went into the light and, ever since he'd felt it, the gnawing blackness of his regret.

"I should have left the bar. I should have left. I should've fallen in love again. I liked the bar, but I should have moved on." Mickey felt a release as he spoke the words aloud for the first time.

"I liked the booze," Stephen said wistfully.

"I know."

"Maybe that's why I can't call my kids, why I live and work up in places like this, why I can't go home. But I regret it, you know, every fucking day I regret it. But then I drink and I forget and then time just passes, it just passes and then it's gone, and then it's been a year and I haven't called and I just... I always come back to it, I guess."

"What?"

"The booze. I think I love it more than I love them, and living up here feels like I'm free to have this grand affair."

Mickey recognized the shame on Stephen's face and pitied him. "You're just drunk," he said, trying to wash it away.

"Aren't we all?" Stephen grasped his side tighter as more blood seeped out. "This cold, it's something else. I love this cold. I bet I would have lived if those fuckers hadn't ganged up on me."

"No, you wouldn't have." Mickey sighed into the cold air.

Stephen stared at him. "You have no breath," he remarked.

Mickey sighed again. "No breath." He rested a hand on Stephen's cold arm.

Stephen's shoulders shook with silent tears. "I need to call my kids, my son. I can book a ticket, I can go home this time. Where's my phone?" He started to thrash around in the snow. "Where's my phone? Where's my coat? I can call, I can go."

"No." Mickey stood and reached his hand out to Stephen, who took hold of it and stood up too.

Stephen gulped air in, then exhaled in a whoosh. "No breath," he said sadly.

"No breath."

"Will I see you again?"

"I don't think so."

"So I'll just be alone then? Up here? In this cold?"

"I dunno. Maybe?"

"Maybe I can walk home. Maybe I can find a drink on the way." Stephen turned and started to walk toward the trees.

Mickey took one last look up at the northern lights, still dancing their eternal dance. The pain in his side was gone completely. The regret he'd been carrying around had faded too. Mickey sighed again and felt himself melt into the darkness.

He wished he didn't have to be alone anymore.

SKIN

As the blue car rounded the side of the gas station, Grace heard the crunch of tires, the squeal of brakes, and the wallowing sounds of Johnny Cash. Her mom, waving erratically from the passenger seat, halted the car in front of Grace and flung her door open. She stepped out of the car, her first few steps languid and flowing, until she tripped on a rock and went jerky. She was dressed in nothing more than a multicoloured satin kimono over Daisy Dukes that had been washed too many times and were all threadbare and faded. Her hands, though, were wrapped in thick pink mittens, a matching toque perched on her head, and her feet were buried in furry pink boots.

"M'girl," she called, her arms outstretched. Grace pulled away as the embrace crushed her shoulders, but her mom leaned in, using Grace to steady hers. "Let me look at you, hey. Oh, Gracie girl."

Her mom's fingers hovered over Grace's face. Tears formed in her eyes, splashing runny black mascara streams down her face. Grace looked away.

"What did they do to you, my beautiful girl, my little girl?"

The car was still running. A man Grace didn't recognize sat in the front seat, thumbing his phone.

"That's just Ron," her mom said as she followed Grace's gaze. "He gave me a ride, I lost my car, hey. But that's okay, Ron there, he drives me when I need to be driven. He's a good man, hey. Little fat, but a good man."

Ron nodded in agreement from the car without looking up. "I'm only fat because she can't cook and we have to eat out all the time."

"I tried cooking."

"You set the curtain above the kitchen sink on fire."

Her mom laughed a loud booming laugh before glancing at Grace's face. "Don't say fire," she said to Ron, her finger hovering over Grace's fresh skin.

Grace sighed. Things with her mom never changed. There was always a Ron. There was always new drama. A new outfit to change into. A new something.

"Get in." Her mom hustled her toward the back seat. "My buns are freezing, and you know us Cree women don't got much bun to begin with."

／

Grace sat on the floral couch in her mom's trailer. The air was dank from the wet laundry hanging off the backs of all the furniture.

"Sorry again about the washing, the dang dryer's been acting up again. Ron fixed it the first time, he says it's my turn this time. What do I know about fixing dryers?"

Grace picked at the plate of KFC on her lap. Her mom had insisted on it because it was a special occasion, even started to cry in the lineup when Grace said she wasn't hungry. So Grace ordered the number two.

Her mom reappeared from the hallway wearing a jet-black wig, the shiny hair down to her knees. She was carrying a box covered in glitter and smudged makeup. Grace put her plate down on the coffee table and groaned. Every time. Every time she visited.

"Makeover time! Meet Candy, my new wig. Ron bought her for me online. Beautiful, isn't she? I wore her to the powwow this summer, I got hit on from all sides." Her mom plopped herself on the couch opposite Grace. "Now, I have some new shades I think could really hide your scars, and this new lipstick that I know will make your eyes pop."

Grace wanted to tell her mom that she didn't want her eyes to pop, that her hoodies worked just fine to hide her scars, that all she wanted was to go for a walk, maybe take some pictures of the trees because she missed them. But her mom was already coming at her with a foundation-soaked makeup sponge.

⟡

Later, Grace—who was standing in the living room so that her mom could curl her hair—asked, "Can Ron drive me back to the gas station?"

"Why, m'girl?"

"Because I need to catch the bus back to the city. I promised Gran I'd be home tonight. They need me."

"That's bullshit," her mom said, and threw down the brush she was holding.

Quiet settled between them. Grace kept her eyes down, focusing on the spilled glitter, the way the light bulb caught the flakes and reflected back light.

"I know you don't—" Her mom walked to the counter, grabbed a piece of fried chicken in one hand and gestured with it. "You never liked it here. Always thought it wasn't good, or cool, or whatever you kids think."

"That's dumb." Grace sank back into the couch. "I needed to live in the city. Gran needed my help. And then." Grace's face burned under the thick layer of concealer.

Her mom put the chicken down and leaned against the counter, her sequined tank top sparkling. "I wanted you here after your accident. I could have taken care of you. I could have... You're my baby, I could have helped you."

Grace never wanted to hurt her mom. She just always seemed to. "I know, but I couldn't leave them."

"I love you, Gracie."

"I know. I love you too."

Her mom smiled and wiped the fat black tear that was dripping off her chin. She stood up and, in a flourish, grabbed a pink scarf from the table. "Well, if you have to leave, you're going to leave in style."

✦

Grace climbed out of Ron's car. "Thanks, Mom. Ron."

Her mom climbed out after her. "You can give me back the shirt when I see you next, but wear it, okay, it's better than that oversized sweater."

Grace nodded, feeling exposed in her mother's clingy red velvet tank top and matching pink scarf. Her makeup was thick and she was freezing. She watched her mom and Ron drive off before pulling her hoodie on over the flashy clothing. As she did, she thought she saw the man in a black T-shirt standing off a ways, staring at her—but when she tried to focus on him again he was gone.

LUNGS

Tommy leaned back on the porch swing. The music from the party inside thumped against the windows of the house. He exhaled into the cool air, watched his breath frost before him. He loved the prickling feeling in his lungs when he inhaled frigid air, because at least he could feel something there. At least he was alive.

The door opened beside him and a waif of a girl slipped out. She settled next to him, a thick blanket wrapped around her shoulders.

"Aren't you freezing?" Laura asked.

"Nah, I like the cold."

"You're going to get sick." She looked at him with wide eyes, guilt and embarrassment pouring from her. "I mean, not like before, not really sick, not like you're going to die or shit. Just like a cold or something."

Tommy winked at her. "Don't worry 'bout me, I'm not about to die sick."

"Tommy, I'm sorry, I'm stupid. I just— I'm happy to see you. You've been hiding since you got home."

"Not hiding. Riding. Different things altogether."

"Your brother, he's been saying—"

"Don't listen to him, I'm fine."

"But you *are* different."

"Am I now?"

"Yeah, like when we were together you were so..."

"What?"

"Impulsive, all over, hard to be around, kinda like."

Tommy grinned as he leaned forward, elbows resting on his knees. "Well, we all grow up sometime, right?"

"It's more than that."

Tommy stopped grinning. "I know. I feel older somehow, like I've lived longer than I should have. I dunno how to explain it. There's so much beauty I never knew existed. Before, I wanted freedom because I just wanted to do this." He waved vaguely at the party inside. "But now I want freedom because I want to explore, I want to see everything. I've been reading." Tommy glanced at her face and saw what he expected: surprise. "I've learned there's so many worlds out there, so many experiences, there's just so much I've been missing."

"So you're going to leave then?"

"As soon as I get some money, yeah. I just have to see it all, you know?"

She shook her head. "Tommy, do you think that if you didn't get sick, we would've..."

"Nah, we would never have lasted," he teased. "But really, I dunno. Maybe."

"Maybe tonight we could just pretend that it's still before. And I never did what I did and you never did you what you did. And that you're not going to leave the island. That we're just the us from before."

Tommy put his arm around her, pulled her close, and sighed. "Nothing ever goes back. Change always happens. But I'm okay with us being who we are now, having done what we did."

Tommy breathed her in. She smelled like lemons. He didn't care. He was only moving forward from now on.

HEART

Quinn pushed a branch aside for Mary Ann, who walked beside him. He'd chosen this trail because it was flat, and because it passed a small pool of water he thought she might like to see, maybe dip her feet in.

When he glanced over, she wore a slight smile, like a flicker of light. He tried to control his breath.

"I'm glad you asked me out." She laughed in her bright way. "Finally."

"Holyyy, there's the sass."

Mary Ann laughed. "I just mean—we've known each other for forever and...I'm just glad."

Quinn felt his face heat up.

He didn't know where the push had come from to finally make a move. All he knew was that he'd felt it in every part of him, a driving need radiating from his centre. And when she'd said yes, he swore he felt someone pat him on the shoulder.

"Hey, there's something I want to show you." He grabbed her hand and led her behind a large boulder. The deep blues and greens of the pool reflected their faces back to them. "It's actually a really nice place to cool off."

Mary Ann flashed a grin before pulling her dress up over her head and running into the water. She laughed with pure joy as she surfaced. "Whatcha waiting for? The water's perfect."

Quinn hesitated, the image of his scarred chest burning through his mind.

"Come on, you brought me here for swimming, right?"

He couldn't help but grin back at her. Mary Ann flipped onto her back to stare at the sky, and he took the opportunity to pull off his T-shirt and shorts before diving in. The coldness of the water only held him in shock for a moment before dissipating. He swam toward Mary Ann and, with a flip of his legs, dove underneath her, popping up on the other side of her languid body. Her long brown hair spread over the surface of the water like millions of threads of love. He swirled his hands through it, felt it cleanse him like the smoke from one of his campfires.

Mary Ann let her feet drop into the water and faced him. "Quinn?"

"Yah?"

"You're better now, right?" She placed her fingertips on his chest. He resisted a flinch.

"I have been reborn," he said with a goofy flourish.

She leaned into him, pressed her lips against his. "Good," she whispered. "Because I'm planning on falling in love with you."

Quinn's whole body felt alive. He wrapped his arms

around her, pulling her even closer to him, and as he inhaled her, he thanked the previous owner of his heart for giving him this chance.

MICKEY

Mickey sat on a brown sofa in a living room. The curtains were closed tight, the air stale and moist. He heard shuffling in another room. He wanted to get up to go see where he was, who he was with, but his head pounded with the stabbing pain he'd still only gotten semi-used to. Instead, he laid his body down on the sofa and reached for the orange throw that was bunched over the top. Lying there, he took in the room's details. Newspapers stacked in the corner by the door. A small kitchen, the counter piled with dirty dishes. A TV on but the volume muted. A La-Z-Boy so worn down the stuffing fluffed out. A pillow balanced on top of a footstool.

Mickey wanted to sleep, to go back to the place of light, but he couldn't, not with the migraine. Not with the buzzing in his ears.

He felt her voice before he heard it.

She was singing, something soft and unrecognizable. It helped the pain, lessened it to a degree where he could crack open the one eye he had left.

He saw her for the first time in the hazy light, as she shuffled out of the back room and into the living room. Her slippers moved over the linoleum in a rough pattern, keeping time with the melody she was humming.

"Now, Doris, what are you going to eat for lunch?" she said to herself. "I dunno, maybe some soup? Not the soup from a can, though. That's all I have. Well, silly woman, maybe you should leave your apartment and go shopping. With all the freaks out there? You're right, plus *Price Is Right* is on soon."

Mickey watched Doris as she puttered about her small kitchen, moving with a familiarity he thought he recognized, though he didn't know where from.

He closed his eye again, falling asleep to her voice as she filled the room with imaginary conversation.

SKIN

"How is your mom?"

Grace looked out the window of her therapist's office. "Fine," she said. "The same, I dunno."

"Did you talk to her about the accident?"

Grace twisted the ends of her hoodie in her hands.

"Grace, you need to start talking about what happened."

"I know what happened."

"Yes, you do. But you also need to heal from it."

Grace pointed to her face. "I thought the doctors were supposed to do that."

"Inner healing, Grace. What happened wasn't your fault."

Grace rolled her eyes at the woman she'd begun calling Ratface in her head. These fucking doctors. None of them knew anything.

"Have you told her yet?"

"Have I told her what?"

Ratface looked uncomfortable. "About what is happening with the graft."

"You mean have I told her about how my face is going to look even more fucked up than before because the new skin is literally rejecting me? And that everything in this fucking world is a joke so she should just focus on all her stupid little trailer-park drama because the big wide world is just so messed up and out to get you so it's better to not even try? Should I really tell her that?"

"Grace, I know you're mad—"

"No, I'm past mad." Grace picked up her backpack and walked to the door. "I'm done."

She slammed the door behind her, ignoring Ratface's calls, and stepped into the spring's warmth.

LUNGS

Tommy felt the bike's vibrations down to his cells. He screamed out his adrenaline into the frosted air.

Suddenly, as he ripped around a corner on the oceanside highway he felt his back tire give way.

Tommy roared.

In that instant, he noticed a man dressed in a black T-shirt and dark jeans standing in the middle of the road ahead.

And then Tommy felt his body crunch—but only for a moment. Then he felt nothing and saw nothing and thought nothing and was nothing.

MICKEY

The boy, Tommy, was crumpled. That was the only way Mickey could describe it. Crumpled into a ball of blood in the middle of the road.

The pavement was black and shiny. The bike smoking hot in the ditch.

Mickey's body ached, screamed in agony. He crouched down, and then he felt breath, real breath again. His chest opened up and he gulped down the air. It was cold but it felt good. He coughed. He shouted, though no one alive could have heard him.

Mickey jumped up. The night had taken on true darkness, yet the moon was bright. He looked back down at Tommy; his hair was spread over his face so Mickey could no longer see his eyes. Mickey closed his eyes and tried to feel Tommy's blood pumping hot through his veins, the way the vibrations of the bike had shaken his teeth—but that was all gone now.

And then he heard a gasp and a cough. He crouched down and instinctively put a hand on Tommy's shoulder.

A voice from behind him. "It was your breath, wasn't it?"

Mickey stood and turned, keeping his eyes down on the pavement, nervous for the first time in a long time.

"And you were watching me?" Tommy asked.

Mickey nodded.

"And all of this, it's your fault?"

Mickey startled. "No, I don't think so."

Tommy's face had changed. He'd lost the worry lines around his eyes, the crease on his forehead. But his eyes, they were still blue and Mickey could almost hear the ocean now when he looked into them.

Tommy nodded as he considered Mickey. His gaze lingering on the patches of missing skin, his empty eye socket, before finally coming to rest on his one good eye.

"So, what now then?"

"I dunno," Mickey answered honestly, sucking in the cold Atlantic air.

"I see you got your breath back." Tommy gestured at Mickey's chest.

"I guess."

Tommy pursed his lips and stared at Mickey. Then he smiled. He leaned his head back and whooped, the sound deep and low. Tommy laughed, doubling over, but never losing his breath. He laughed until some of the ocean had leaked its way down his face. And then he grinned at Mickey before turning around and running down the road in the direction he'd been headed on his bike.

Mickey watched him, listened to the laughter until the waves consumed the sound, Tommy growing fainter and fainter, swallowed by the forest shadows.

EYE

Doris poured herself another bowl of cereal. She wasn't supposed to eat it because of the sugar, but she'd given up caring years earlier. Nothing truly bad had happened, other than diabetes getting her eye, but they'd given her a new one, so no harm done. And she almost felt grateful it had gone, because the new one let her see the world differently. It cut away some of the harshness that the original eye had been too focused on.

She'd always been a quiet person. And not for any traumatic reason either, like one might suppose. It was just her way.

Her job, before she retired, was one of solitude, plugging away at numbers in a distant cubicle in one corner of a big office where everyone secretly hated each another. Except for Doris—she'd never formed a distinct opinion of anyone. And no one who worked there even noticed she existed. No one ever spoke to her other than by email for years. Eventually she stole her computer and stopped going to the office. She started working from home. Then one day there was no one at the other end of an email, just an out of office: *we're totally bankrupt and yeah, sorry* auto response. She supposed she might have known about the impending end if she'd still been in the office.

So she retired. She had enough money saved to live her life until she died. She rented, she didn't have a car, no kids, no husband, she already had a TV and all the furniture she'd ever need, she never left the house except for her weekly grocery shop, and even that was becoming less and less necessary with the internet taking over.

It would be dishonest to say that Doris never felt lonely. That, deep inside, she never craved another human's touch. But she'd gotten used to clamping down that feeling as soon as it rose in her. Instead she turned her mind toward her friends on the TV, because in the most real way, they were her friends. She didn't think they were real, she wasn't that far gone, but their company was dependable.

After she got her new eye, though, things had changed. She started to feel a restless energy. An itch that demanded she leave the comforting walls of her apartment and travel to a town she had never heard of before, the name of which had suddenly come to her in a dream. The town was called Lily's Lake. She thought the name was too sentimental to be real, but she'd looked it up. It was real and in the north, far north. Why would she travel that far for no reason?

But as the nights passed, she began to form a picture in her mind of the place. There was something about it. Something she needed to see.

HEART

Quinn stroked the skin on Mary Ann's back, felt the way her breath pushed past muscle. Marvelled at the expanse of her bare skin. For the hundredth time, he sent a silent prayer up to the stars for allowing him to know her like this. Their time together had been more than Quinn could have imagined. Once he let go of his fear, once he leaned into her, it had been so easy, so much easier than anything in his life had been. He sighed as he lay back down beside her.

It was then that his heartbeat squeezed, erratic. A few beats off rhythm, for just a moment. Then longer.

He coughed, flexing his diaphragm, trying to coax his heart back into proper time. He started to feel a slight heaviness, so he focused on his breath.

He had a new heart. He had a better heart. He was beating in time. He was okay.

Mary Ann stirred beside him. "What's wrong?"

"Nothing, just a tickle in my throat. Go back to sleep."

She turned to face him, her eyes squinted with concern. "You sure?" She laid a gentle hand on his chest, on the scar over his heart.

He threaded his fingers through hers. "I'm fine. Kisâki-hitin."

She nuzzled into his chest. "I love you too," she whispered, slipping back into her dreams.

Quinn concentrated on his breath, willing his heart to reset. Willing life to fill him with vitality, willing for this moment to continue forever.

SKIN

Grace groaned. The fluorescent lights of the hospital buzzed overhead as she writhed in pain. Tears leaked out of her eyes as she waited for the nurse to pump more drugs into her system. When they hit her bloodstream, she felt them almost immediately: first a ball of nausea in the pit of her stomach, then a slight fluttering through her nervous system, and finally the weight of her body becoming numb.

Her eyelids fluttered as she fought to keep them open for a few more minutes. There was a man. She scrunched her face and squinted her eyes, trying to make the world come into focus again, until she couldn't keep her eyes open any longer and finally succumbed to their closing.

But she didn't sleep. She drifted there between life and death, or so she imagined, caught in some fuzzy faraway place with colours shooting like a meteor shower behind her eyelids.

Someone sat on the end of her bed. She felt the mattress shift and move.

"Whooo's there?" she murmured.

A hand rested gently on her leg. Lemons, the tart sweetness of summer, filled the air.

"Why-y-y are you f-f-following me?" she asked. The drugs caused her words to slur, to dribble down her chin.

Before the person—she knew it was a man wearing a black T-shirt and jeans, even though she couldn't see him—could answer, she heard the fast and hard footsteps of her doctor.

The doctor's fingers pressed into her skin, all business as he checked her over.

She remembered how he'd tried to remind her, when she first came screaming into the emergency room, that the cadaver skin was only supposed to be temporary, that eventually it would be removed and skin from own her thigh would be put in its place, and that the only thing she could focus on was how he was too beautiful to be a doctor who looked at ugliness every day. She'd yelled at him that this was his fault, that if he had done the graft properly, if he had *fixed* her properly, if he had done his fucking job, she wouldn't be here, she would be at home painting with a not-as-disgusting, oozing, black-because-the-flesh-is-rotting-and-falling-off face.

She no longer had the energy to yell. And when she heard him whispering to another doctor about how she needed to get to surgery immediately, she felt a stab of pain inside, somewhere deep, somewhere the drugs couldn't numb.

The hand on her leg squeezed in reassurance, and for a moment, she felt relief. At least she wasn't alone.

MICKEY

Mickey could feel Doris more than he could the others.

He whispered to her at night while she slept. He told her all about his bar. The way the counter glistened in the light after everyone had left. How the sunshine on his T-shirt would melt into him and make him feel so good and warm and gooey. How he would always light the candles his sister made for him, lemon and lavender ones, while he did his paperwork in the morning.

He whispered to her everything he'd ever wanted to say to someone he loved. And she always listened.

HEART

Quinn's chest felt like a weight had settled onto it. Heavy and tight. His body was constricting, strangling the soul inside of his flesh. Mary Ann sat beside him, her forehead cut with lines of worry like an inland waterway. He gripped her fingers with his as his breath came in shallow spurts.

He'd woken up in the middle of the night, weeks after

the first squeezing in his chest, dawn still hours away, to intense pain—pain that stole his breath and replaced it with a scratchy wheeze. Mary Ann called the ambulance as she soon as she realized what he didn't, or rather couldn't, tell her, which was of course that he was dying.

He had known for a few weeks he was dying. He couldn't pinpoint how he knew; it was more a general feeling.

That, and the woodpecker.

The first time it visited was while he was reading, with a little peck of a beak against the window pane.

The second time, he was outside in Mary Ann's garden wrestling thick weed roots from the rich dark soil. The bird landed beside him on the edge of the planter box and deliberately pecked into the soft wood. Quinn let it peck, because who was he to dismiss a messenger?

He'd hoped, though, that the bird would give him more time before visiting again. He wanted more time with Mary Ann. But he guessed, rather accurately, it turned out, that just wasn't meant to be. And now she was here beside him in the hospital. A place she didn't belong.

The woodpecker's third visit—the death sentence visit, as his grandmother liked to say—had happened in the dusk light that night. She hadn't noticed the woodpecker, it had flown by so fast, but if she had seen it she'd have known, or at least guessed. She knew the same stories he did. Three visits from a woodpecker, death's messenger, and you'd soon be at a funeral. He desperately wished again for it not to be his funeral.

Quinn closed his eyes against the fluorescent lights, against her worried gaze and mournful tears. He wanted to spare Mary Ann as much pain as possible. If he could handle his heart rotting in his chest, he could handle this goodbye too and make it the easiest he could for her.

MICKEY

Mickey sat with Quinn in the hospital. The light was muted. The heavy beige drapes filtered out everything but the strongest rays. Quinn hurt. Mickey could feel it in his own body. All over, a heavy pain, one that came from his centre and, like tendrils of smoke, curled around every part of him.

Quinn's eyes were closed, his breathing laboured. He'd been in the hospital for so long that Mickey knew it meant he was never going to leave. Mickey felt a prick in his remaining eye, like a tear wanted to escape but didn't know how.

Quinn was too young, Mickey thought. They all had been. Maybe everyone was, ultimately.

Mary Ann had left earlier to go to work. She'd missed too many shifts, Quinn had suggested, and he told her to go because he didn't want anything to happen to her. Mickey suspected that Quinn just didn't want her to see him die. His final act, one of love.

"Do you think the Creator will grant me access to the sky?"

Mickey looked up from Quinn's bed. Quinn was sitting on the window ledge, watching Mickey and his own now-dead body. Mickey stood up and walked toward him.

"If you ask, maybe."

"You haven't asked?"

"I don't know how to, I guess."

Quinn nodded before looking down at his hands. "I just want to make sure she's okay, you know?"

"I know." And Mickey did; he felt it in every beat of the heart that was now back in his chest. "Thank you." Mickey didn't know how to fully thank Quinn. Nothing felt like enough.

Quinn smiled at Mickey. "Just promise me you'll ask when you figure out how."

Mickey gripped Quinn's shoulder and gave it a squeeze before turning to the light. "You coming?" Mickey asked.

"I'm going to stay for a while, I think. I want to be here when she gets back. Maybe I'll be able to stay... like you did. Maybe she'll be able to see me too."

"Good luck, Quinn. I'll see you around."

Mickey left Quinn and moved into the light and nothingness. He put his hand on his heart, his beating heart, now infused with more love than he'd ever known.

EYE

The bar smelled like lemons and lavender.

Doris stepped into the centre of the room. It looked like she'd imagined it would. She had been dreaming of the bar for months. And now she was here, and it was real. The trip to Lily's Lake had been a nightmare, but one that dimmed the closer she got. As the trees got fuller and the sky expanded, she felt a calm enter her body, and she leaned into it until she actually began to enjoy herself. She hadn't really been out of her apartment for years.

Above the bar hung a picture of a man dressed in a black T-shirt, dark jeans, bearing a small downturned smile.

Doris slid into a seat, and a woman in her forties came out from the back. She looked surprised to see Doris.

"Bar isn't open yet. We're not serving drinks till after four."

"That's okay, I just want to sit here for a while." The woman looked like she was going to protest, so Doris kept speaking. "The man in the picture, who is he?"

The woman's smile stretched her face open. "My brother Mickey. This is, or was, his bar."

"What happened to him?"

"He died."

"And you kept the bar?" Doris didn't know where the questions were coming from, but she had to know.

"He wanted me to. I made him a promise. He loved this place."

"Mickey's Bar."

"Mickey's Bar. Although I'm thinking of calling it Stacy's Bar now."

Doris felt laughter bubble up from an invisible place inside of her. "I think he would be okay with that."

"I don't know, he was very particular."

Doris looked around. "You got rid of the fluorescent lights."

"What?"

"They're gone."

"Have you been here before?"

"No. I just feel like I have, or maybe I dreamed it." Doris didn't know what else to say. "What was Mickey like?"

Stacy let out the loud laugh of someone who has grieved a person and loves them even more now because of that grief. "Mickey opened this bar in his early twenties, when he was still a kid, really. He didn't know what to do with his life, so he left the farm where we grew up, got in his truck, and just drove. I guess he drove until he hit this town and stopped, and he never left." Stacy was caught up in her memories. "He never told me why he stopped here, or why he stayed." Stacy flicked her pen a few times as the silence filled between them. "He died here, you know."

Doris nodded. She didn't know how but she knew.

"He loved this place. I just had to keep it, you know?"

"Love." Doris stared up at the picture of Mickey. "Don't know it."

"You should try it some time. It's the only thing that makes life worth a damn."

"Maybe." Doris smiled a sad smile. There wasn't much of a chance to fall in love in her apartment. And she was happy alone—she always told herself she was.

"Here." Stacy poured her a drink, a whisky. "For Mickey."

Doris thought she saw a flicker beside Stacy—Mickey, the man in the photo wearing a black T-shirt smiling a smile so wide it stretched his face. Doris held her glass up to the picture. She didn't know why, but in that second, she felt happiness in every part of her. And something else—something that maybe felt like love. And then the flicker of the man was gone.

MICKEY

Mickey watched with sorrow as Grace—wonderful, quiet, artistic Grace—slipped below the surface of the raging water. He thought she might scramble for one final gasp of air but she just disappeared.

"The cold felt good, surprisingly." Grace crouched beside Mickey on the riverbank. Her fingers churned the earth as her eyes stayed fixed on the water. "I thought it was going to hurt, burn my skin."

"You didn't have to," he said. Even as he spoke, he knew he was wrong to say it. Who was he to judge?

"I didn't, but I wanted to." Grace stood and looked at him. Her face was healed—she looked like she was always supposed to. "I just couldn't hurt my mom anymore. She tried so hard for so long to get where she is. I was only prolonging her pain, everyone's pain. It was never going to get better." She began to walk away from him, her shoulders slumped.

"Grace—"

She turned for a moment. "Thanks for being here. And thanks for loaning me your skin." Grace gave him a half smile before walking away into nothingness.

Mickey looked down at his body. His skin was once again whole. He could feel the wind against it, the way it moved over him like velvet, but he didn't feel joyful for its return. He only felt loss.

EYE

Doris returned from her trip radiating joy. The travelling itch was gone. She moved back into her life's routine and was happy for it.

Something was different, though: she felt a contentment she'd always wished for but never fully had. She wasn't lonely anymore.

MICKEY

Doris seemed like she would live forever.

Mickey would watch her from the stool in the corner of their room. He watched her as she slept, as she got up to pee, as she settled back into bed and turned on the TV, as she ate perched on the edge of her bed with a book in her hand, as she lived every day in her apartment. He sat and watched and willed her to keep living.

Mickey wanted Doris to live forever, so much so that he ached. His heart remembered Quinn, the way Quinn felt love. Mickey finally understood that though he may have been alone when he died, in death, love could still blossom.

In Doris's shitty apartment—in between commercial breaks, in the moments when they sat in silence together gazing down at the people on the street, when he lay beside her in bed watching her breath slip between her lips, her lips that he longed to run his fingertips over—he felt all the love he never had.

After Doris brought him back to the bar, that was when he knew it was okay to say goodbye to it and to everything it represented. Because he'd found a new place to call home.

❧

After a time, the world started to grow blurry.

Sometimes, while watching TV with Doris, things would shift or fall, and he'd be thrown off balance by the tilt-a-whirl of age and time. When that happened, Doris would clutch her head, her fragile fingers curled around the spotted skin covering her skull.

Other times, Mickey would feel a burst of not-quite-pain strike him in his empty eye socket. He would disappear, and only come back after Doris was asleep. His heart ached for the moments he lost with her.

❧

Mickey sat holding Doris's hand most of the time now, willing her to keep breathing.

Then came the day when she did finally see him, and Mickey wished with everything that she couldn't.

Doris stared at Mickey, who was sitting beside her on the bed. He held her frail fingers, tracing a flower pattern onto her skin.

"It's you." Her voice was weak, but Mickey knew it better than he knew his own.

"Hi." Mickey's eyes clouded with unshed tears.

"I could..." Doris coughed.

Mickey knew it was almost over. He tried to use his grip to tether her to the earth.

"I could smell you, did you know that," she whispered. "At night. You smell like lemons, sometimes lavender."

Mickey's vision was fading. He gripped her hand harder. "Doris."

He didn't know what to say. So many of his words had spilled out of him over their shared pillows for years, but now—now he didn't know what to say.

Doris gripped his hand back. "I know."

Mickey's vision cleared. Doris's breathing had stopped.

And then he heard her humming, something gentle and soft, behind him. He felt her hand on his shoulder, her fingers as they traced the lines on his neck.

"I never felt alone," she whispered into his ear.

"Neither did I." He swivelled around to look at her. And for the first time he could see his love reflected back to him.

She slipped her arms around him, buried her face into his shoulder, and he held her. The woman who had changed him without meaning to. He closed his eyes and breathed her in, and even though he couldn't say anything, it was everything.

/

Once again, Mickey was in a place of light.

Not fluorescent light; he couldn't see the paunchy globs under his eyes or the hunch in his shoulders, and he wondered briefly if they'd ever existed at all. He prodded his empty eye socket and found it full once more. Mickey looked down at himself.

Mickey was full. Mickey was whole. Mickey was Mickey.

He patted each organ, each person he'd spent his life with. And he realized, Mickey was more.

Mickey was ready.

STRAIGHT TALK FROM THE STRAIGHTEST OF SHOOTERS

Don't let anyone ever tell you you can't do that thing you want to do so badly you can't stand it. Don't let them tell you you can't slide through it to the other side. Don't let the throbbing in your temples stop you from becoming who you're meant to be. Don't let me tell you anything you don't want to know.

Turn off the TV, it hates you anyway, it just wants you to buy stupid shit you'll just end up giving away to the poor-people store in a few years anyway. They don't need any more shitty, half-broken, stained-with-your-juices junk.

But don't listen to me.

By all means, go sit in front of your monstrous flat screen, let it bathe you in blue light. Let the laughter of all those identical fucking actors wash over you, and let yourself forget that nobody likes you, really.

Let the comforting notion that you at least made it through a few more hours lull you into something like sleep. Except you don't really sleep anymore, do you? You just lie there, unconscious but not falling into the rhythm of that thing we're supposed to do, you know the one—the rapid eye movement and the deep sleep and the restorative sleep and your-brain-cataloguing-things sleep.

Wake up, look at your phone, like things until you like yourself, or hate yourself, or figure out how to improve yourself.

But don't listen to me. I hate myself more than you like your frenemies.

IN REMEMBRANCE

The old man and his old wife shuffled along the corridor of their shitty apartment building. It smelled like week-old farts. They clutched hands, each making sure the other didn't fall because he had that bad hip, and she had that bad ankle from falling on the ice, back when their kids were still alive.

Just as they reached the door to their apartment, a cough seeped out from the neighbour's apartment. His door always sat half open, even in the middle of night. A hand reached out of the door and gripped the wood frame.

The old woman called out, in a voice that was surprisingly forceful, "I'm making cabbage rolls for dinner."

Moe, the man who lived next door, stepped into the gap between the door and frame. His hair was dyed an obvious burgundy and sat in a poof on top of his wrinkled head. He nodded in acknowledgement to the old couple as they slipped into their apartment.

The air inside was heavy and thick—moist, more like it, with condensation running in rivulets down their windows. The old man detached his hand from his wife's. Unattached, he shuffled a bit faster as he went to lay his bag onto the already cluttered kitchen table. The logo of their business, which they'd owned for more than fifty years, stared up at him: *Loving Mortuary.*

The old woman took her coat off and hung it on the rack by the door. Her thin arms snaked out from her oversized black sweater.

When they'd started the business, the old man recalled, his wife was full of colour, and dressed in pinks, blues, yellows, greens. But then the business had stopped doing well—too many dead people in the world, but not enough where they lived. And then they'd gone through the worst thing a parent could. And she had changed. The colourful dresses had disappeared into the closet and had stayed there, jammed against the wall.

The old man moved to his green armchair in their living room. It was adjacent to the kitchen, so he could still see his wife as she started to pull cabbage from the fridge, but not so close that he would be required to help. If asked, he would, but he really didn't want to. He needed to think. He was in trouble. They were in trouble, his wife and himself, and he didn't quite know what to do about it.

Before long, the door to their apartment squeaked open, and a claw-like hand gripped the frame before a body pushed through it. Moe huffed into the room, leaving the door slightly ajar.

"So, you hear the news?" Moe was always the first to know anything. "That new gal, the blond bodybuilder in 2A. She lost her case."

"What's going to happen now?" The old woman looked up from the game of solitaire she was playing while dinner simmered in the oven.

"They're giving full custody to the grandmother, father's side."

"That poor girl." The old woman pulled the cards together to make room for Moe at the table.

"I heard her all afternoon, making such a racket, you wouldn't believe it. She was throwing things—plates, I think."

The old woman tsked. "That's why she lost the poor thing, that temper."

"Ah, you can't tell anyone nothing anymore, or else I would've told her to straighten up months ago. But you know how it goes."

"I do."

"And you? How's your heart?" the old woman inquired to be polite.

"Still murmuring some, but the doc says it's nothing to be worried about. He says he's more worried about my shoulder."

"What's wrong with your shoulder?"

As they sat and chatted, the old man remained in his green armchair, slightly apart. He was lost, half in deep thought, half close to a nap—he was quite old, after all. His chair was moulded to his body by this point, shorter than the man's, sure, but perhaps destined to continue long after.

He was roused from his liminal state by his wife's loud voice. "Dinner's ready," she exclaimed once, and then again when the old man failed to fully wake.

When he did finally move, it was with a series of creaks and groans, all of which only served to remind him of everything disintegrating in his body—something he should have been wholly aware of after having taken care of so many decomposing bodies in his lifetime. But alas, they don't tell you how foreign your body becomes as you age. His mind, when he could keep everything straight, still believed he was thirty-three, but his body felt even older than ninety-two.

"Come to the table now, sit, we're starving." His wife's voice was as bossy as it'd ever been, and this warmed him and made him move slightly faster.

Moe held a dripping cabbage roll over his plate, eyeing the old man through his busy eyebrows. "I can see you have something on your mind," he said. He stated this as a fact.

The old man debated lying, but Moe always knew everyone's business—sometimes before even they did—so what was the point?

"I'll figure it out," the old man replied.

"Perhaps," said Moe.

The old man felt himself angering. Who was Moe to know his business? But when he turned to his wife, he could see the strain around her eyes. She hated when he got angry. So he forced his words down and took a deep breath instead. "This is lovely, sweetheart," he said. His voice came out weaker than expected.

"For you, always." Her cheeks were rosy with the compliment. Her rosy blushing cheeks were one of the reasons he'd fallen in love with her.

Moe slurped back the sauce. His own companion, another old man, had died four years prior. This old man and his wife had prepared the body for no charge.

The trio continued to eat their meal in the kind of steady silence that comes to people used to eating together. When each was full, they sat back, bursting with the sedating effects of a delicious meal.

The old woman was just about to ask if anyone was interested in cake when the door to the apartment flew open. The doorknob hit the wall with such force that the drywall caved in with a little sigh. A man younger than all of them bounded into the apartment. He wore black pants and a black T-shirt, sneakers the colour of blood, with a matching blood-red jacket thrown around his shoulders. In his fist he held what looked like a small bat, something that the old man was certain could be used to hurt someone. The old man was also certain that the bat had been brought to harm him in particular.

In a move straight from a movie, Moe grabbed his cleared dinner plate from the table and hit the intruder over the head with such force that the man stumbled into the nearest wall.

The intruder began crying, and uttering sad, garbled words. The old man assumed it was practised, something the intruder had intended to say to the three of them—or at the very least to him—but before the young man could recover, Moe picked up a shard of the plate and stabbed him in the throat. A fountain of blood poured down his front, saturating his T-shirt and then his pants before mingling with the red of his sneakers. The young man fell dead face down before them.

In the shocked silence, no one said a thing.

Moe returned to the table. His fingers were trembling and his energy from the delicious dinner was sapped. The old man knew Moe had been in World War II as a younger man, and he suspected that what he'd just seen—Moe, acting first—was the reason he'd survived when so many hadn't.

The old woman got up from the table, stumbling on her shaky legs, and closed the still-open door. Then she went and leaned on her husband, who was braced against the wall.

The old man knew him. The body on the floor. He was the very reason the old man had been lost so deep in thought before dinner.

"Moe...what have you done?" The old woman looked to Moe, but he was in shock. "Who is this man?" his wife shouted.

Moe couldn't speak yet; his fingers were still trembling. The old man imagined his heart was as well.

The old man now had a choice: should he tell the truth or should he continue to lie?

Moe made the decision for him. "Marty," Moe finally uttered in a whisper, "I think you should tell her."

For a second, the old man was shocked—how had Moe known?—but then he sighed, because Moe knew everything about everyone.

The old man looked up into his wife's face. The delicate wrinkles that fanned out from her eyes creased all the way to her hairline as she focused wholly on him. "A few years ago..." He paused. How could say this? "The business was— We weren't doing well."

"We've never done well," she whispered in a voice tight with fear.

"We really weren't doing well. Worse than now."

"Why didn't you say anything to me?" she yelled again.

"Because tending the dead brings you joy. How could I?" he said meekly.

And that was true. His wife loved their business tremendously. Talking to the dead, helping them understand they were dead, that was her unparalleled gift. When they'd grown old enough to retire, they hadn't, she'd felt such a burden of responsibility for the poor souls on their metal tables.

Her face was drained of all blood as she stared at the body on the floor. "And so who is this?"

The old man hung his head in shame. "I give him the cremated remains of our clients. He turns them into chalk for his art."

This dead man had been a client of theirs years ago, when his mother had passed. A mediocre artist who dreamed of creating work so admired by the world that his name would be like a god, drowned in praise and wonder. One evening— or so he told the old man—he'd flung everything in his studio around in a rage, and his mother's cremated remains, sitting for so long inside a small cardboard box, spilled out onto the floor. He was seized then with an urgency to preserve them forever, and on an impulse mixed the remains with his usual chalk recipe. When he finally gained the nerve to use the chalk, it produced with such accuracy the colour of his mother's despair that he wept uncontrollably in front of his work. When he showed the piece to colleagues, they too were overcome by emotion.

And so, months after taking his mother's remains home, he contacted the old man about possibly obtaining other people's remains—for art, the purest of endeavours. And the old man had been curious—and desperate. So when the man handed him an envelope filled with cash, the old man handed back a small baggie containing a portion of ashes from a young child with a fondness for lemons. The work that resulted now hung in a prominent gallery, a rope separating it from the public. It was much admired. So too was the one made from the ashes of a young man so consumed with jealously that he'd killed his business partner before turning the gun on himself—its emerald colour so deep it made people rip out their hair just to have it. That one sat behind glass so thick even the security guards couldn't get at it. It remains sealed off from everyone, forever.

When the old man was done with his explanation, he expected anger or confusion. He expected a slap to the face; he expected incredulous silence. Anything but what he got, which was his wife's hand under his chin, tilting his face up, a soft kiss. "You always take care of me," she said, absolving her husband of his guilt just like that.

The old man was grateful for her acceptance. But truly he knew his wife had always seen the world differently than what was expected, had always seen death even more differently, knowing that it wasn't the end but the start of our souls' journey.

"Well, I guess people have to make art out of something," Moe said, finding his voice. He stood up and walked back over the body. He reached down and, with delicate fingers, pulled the man's wallet from the back of his jeans. "We might need this later," he said as an afterthought, though the old man suspected he just wanted to know more about the dead man. "I don't know about you two, but I think we should do something about this fellow before the flies start setting up camp." Now that his shock was wearing off, Moe was all business.

The old woman looked back down to the body. "But why was he here tonight? And why was he so angry?"

"Because there are so many fewer people in our ovens these days. He says ours is the only funeral home that produces ashes the way he needs." The old man had long suspected it was his wife and her gift of talking to the dead as she prepared them that made the ashes so transcendent.

Moe spoke again. "People want eco-friendly burials now. Where do they come up with this stuff? I want to be a willow, I want to be a cedar tree, I want my body to feed a whole forest. More like bugs," he spat.

"What does this mean for us?" she asked. "Can we stay open?"

"No. He paid our rent. He used to cover our lights and water too, but since there's been less to give him—"

"So we need money."

Moe stretched his arms over his head before resting his hands on his bony hips. "You have money, right there." He used his foot to point to the man.

"We can't rob him."

"I'm not talking about robbing him, I'm talking about using him."

They stared at him, expectantly.

"Let's turn him into chalk." He gestured to the old woman. "I've seen your drawings. You could use the chalk, we could sell the work."

The old woman had no idea how Moe had seen her drawings. They were secreted in books beneath the floorboards. Not even her husband had seen them.

The old man and the old woman regarded each other. But not in shock; they hadn't been truly shocked at anything since their twins, Hazel and Arron, had died from meningitis when they were five and a half. After losing their children, everything else in life had lost most of its meaning—even this.

The old woman asked, "How will we get him to the ovens?"

The old man added, "Do any of us know how to make chalk? Where we would sell it?"

Moe was already at the front door, his hand on the knob. "Just a few moments." He opened the door slightly and slipped though. "I'll have the solution to our problem," he continued before shutting the door again.

Moe had always had a loose definition of morals. Throughout the long years they'd been neighbours and friends, he had become their confidant, their family. He had been there, in the next apartment, when their babies had passed, had filled their kitchen with chatter and distraction since. Year after year, as youth fled from all three of them. It was only fitting he was here with them now.

Moe re-entered the apartment not too much later, the angry girl from 2A trailing behind him. Her eyes widened slightly at the blood, but she remained. The old man and the old woman eyed each other worriedly, but Moe was already digging through the man's jacket. He pulled out a set of keys.

"Trish here is going to help us move the body. This guy has a car parked out front. We're going to move him in it to the home, then Trish and I are going to sell the car to a man I know who'll pay us in cash. Trish is going to keep that cash."

The old woman extended a hand toward Trish. "Would you like some cake, dear, before we get started? We were just about to eat dessert."

Trish narrowed her eyes but took the old woman's hand. "I'll help you."

While Trish and the old woman were in the kitchen, Moe turned to the old man. "You two are going to do what you do and turn him into ash. I'll go to his apartment and collect his supplies."

"Are you sure—"

"Trust me. Trish is just as desperate as we are. She needs cash to get her kid. We can do this," Moe said before covering the body in a blanket from the sofa.

/

The old woman was alone in the cold morgue with the dead man, washing his limbs, though she really didn't have to. The loading and unloading of the body, the selling of the car, and the gathering of the chalk-making supplies was surprisingly easy. The now-dead man had lived alone. No one to miss him, no one to ask questions.

He spoke from behind her. "I got that tattoo when I was eighteen. I saved up for it for three years."

The old woman brushed the cloth against the black lines. "It's beautiful." And it was. She had seen many tattoos in her lifetime, most of them meaningless in death. This one pulsed with love. "What does it mean?"

"Life."

"But not yours?"

"No, my sister's. She died when she was a baby. My mom hadn't named her yet, so she was buried unmarked. I always wanted her life to be remarked on, so I marked it myself."

"I'm sorry for what we have to do here, but my husband, he's set on it, I'm afraid."

"And you?"

"I trust him." She pushed his hair back. "Such lovely features. Did anyone love you?"

The man came to stand on the other side of the table. He stared down at his own body. "No."

"But did you love someone?"

"No. I did try to make the whole world fall in love with me, though. I thought being an artist would do that, but my work is nothing. I know that now."

"But your paintings hang all over the world."

"It's not my work they love, it's yours."

"My work?"

"This." His palm hovered above hers. "You made the ashes what they were."

Tears pricked the old woman's eyes. She felt such sadness for him. She knew that many of the people on her table never achieved what they wanted. Were never loved by those they wanted. Didn't have people crying over them. But he was different—he was truly the most alone person she'd ever met.

"Make me into something," he whispered to her, as if he could read her mind. "Make people fall in love with me. Make the whole world fall in love with me."

❧

In the light of the afternoon sun, the old woman stepped back from the board. She rested the nubbin of black chalk against the wood of the easel, saving the last remnants for herself. She heard an intake of breath as her husband entered the room, a clatter of boxes as he dropped the pamphlets to the ground.

"Sweetheart, it's—"

"Beautiful?" she whispered.

"It's love." He gathered her in his arms while keeping his eyes fixated on the canvas.

The old woman too looked upon her work with blurry eyes. A replica of the dead man's tattoo, transformed. Her heart swelled, overwhelmingly so, and she knew that she'd succeeded.

Love.

This piece of art was it. Her reason. Her breath. Her life. She detached her husband's arms from her shoulders and took her place on the stool in front of it. Her eyes glowing with tears as she fondly caressed the edges of the canvas. The sounds of her husband faded, every memory she had, every scrap of life she'd lived—nothing else compared to this. Nothing else mattered.

This was true love.

THIRTEEN STEPS

Ringed, red, puffy, and swollen—tired eyes—my eyes. Reflected in a worn spoon held between trembling fingers, cold in the darkness of this final morning—my final morning. The spoon clangs as it hits the floor. The darkness swallows it. I stare into the flickering candle. I squeeze my hands into fists. Bacon, eggs, toast with jam. Coffee, two scoops of sugar, always. Always. The last time. A shiver runs up my spine; my breath catches in my chest.

I remember the air—cold and icy—it was early-morning air. The kind of air that makes you wonder if you've already died, if you're already standing before the oarsmen waiting to be taken to the afterlife. It burned my lungs—this air, it burned and it felt good. The tall grass field was covered in a fine mist that was starting to burn off in the dawn's weak light. It was beautiful, I remember. I was tired; my eyes were closing every few steps. To kill on that perfect morning. My toes curled as the cold wrapped around them. The birds hadn't yet stirred.

My eyes find the plate in front of me. A white plate with a chip on the edge. Silence. No one shares this prison with me. Yolk the

I headed toward the grove of trees that lived behind the farm, on to the hill that looks over the plain. One step and then another, my pattern of daisies. A silent bouquet. The colour of that dress—that yellow dress she wore, my mother. She wore that dress, that yellow dress. When? She wore her yellow dress, that egg-yolk dress to my birthday. That birthday, twenty years ago, with the lemon-and-lavender cake, that lemon-and-lavender cake that melted onto my tongue. With all that frosting, smooth and deep. I had to dig to find the cake. There were smiles in the sun, in the afternoon, smiles from me, from Mary and Peter, from my mother in her yellow dress. Her yellow dress, swaying in the breeze, swirling around her legs.

feet—they brought me to the tree line. It was dark in the grove. I could barely see. It was too cold and I should have turned back. But I had to hunt. We needed meat. I had to, it wasn't my choice. I had to go out and meet the mist. My stomach clenched in hunger around the little bit of water I'd sipped before slipping out the door. Filling emptiness with emptiness.

Coffee spills down my chin—burns. My hands, they won't stop shaking. The cell is filling with grey light and my hands, they won't stop shaking. The cold, there was the cold, there was the cold, and I should have turned back. In the darkness

It was so dark in there, in the forest—on that morning more so than any other morning. I can't explain how the murk of the mist seeping through the dead leaves and forgotten animal tracks held me still. I can only remember how in my

I didn't know, I couldn't see, I didn't know. I grab my fork and force cold eggs down my throat. The candle is almost gone; the flame is sputtering. I tried speaking at the trial, but my words were like dust, choking and gagging me. What I wanted to, needed to, wanted to, should have said. I should have said that we needed the meat. That no one was willing to help us anymore. I should have said anything instead of nothing, but how would they listen to anything I said after what I'd done. And Peter. I imagine his eyes, they look at me from across the cell. In this dim morning light even they turn from me and cast themselves onto my shaking hands, still stained by the memory of gunpowder and blood.

The guard with the runny nose and dirty sleeve walks by. He's Peter's age, almost a man. Peter, who is afraid of the dark, who wears my

stillness the world was also completely still. We held our breath, the woods and I, we held our breath and we waited. In that darkness nothing was pressing, nothing in my life was real. He wasn't real. In that darkness my feet, my toes, they were curled in the cold, pressed against the leather of my boots and around the wool of my socks. And then a rustle, a rustle and the crack of a branch, a rustle, the crack of a branch, and then an exhale of breath. I froze, listening. My heart pounded and I pulled the gun up. The weight in my hands. The blood in my ears. Straining to hear beyond the sound of my own adrenaline.

The smooth metal barrel. I'd crept into Peter's room and borrowed his gun that morning. The crack of the branch, the infinite echo.

thick black coat to bed to keep the fear at bay. Peter, who won't look me in the eye anymore. The guard walks by again, head down, eyes averted. No one will look me in the eye anymore. But they don't know; they don't know how dark it was that morning. They can't know. I am tempted to reach out to the guard, to have the feeling of another human on my skin before I go, but I clutch my fingers around my plate instead.

One eye closed. The smooth metal barrel soft and cold against my cheek. The weight in my hands familiar but distant, a memory: my father teaching me to shoot at wild turkeys, holding me against him as he steadied my arm, taught my aim. Killing as we needed to. We always have to kill when we need to. And I needed to today. And I need to tomorrow. Killing will always need to be done. By me. By someone.

My toast drops. Silent on the rock floor. The cold curls around my toes. My toes, like my sister's. She said we had the same toes, that day by the river when the heat was thick. When our feet were sweating so we took off our shoes and walked into the river. Mary. She smiled and pointed at our feet. Our toes: the same. That summer there was only the heat and our toes in the river.

I searched for the rustle, the noisemaker. My brother's rifle a weight in my hands. If only the sun was up higher; if only I had a candle. If only Peter had woken up before me, had taken his gun. If only I had gone back to bed. If only I hadn't been alone. If only I wasn't always alone.

Are you going to finish your breakfast? The words push out of the guard's mouth. His eyes are staring at the floor. His nose runs. No one will look me in the eye. My fingers find my plate, cold stiff bacon. He walks away. He wants me to finish. He wants the sun to finish rising. He wants me to walk the thirteen steps.

In a few minutes I will walk through the grey light, through the cold building, into the barren courtyard. My stomach clenches around the undigested egg yolk and salty bacon. A walk where no one will look me in the eye. They won't know, can't know, about the silence of that morning. The dark and the cold.

Another rustle. I saw it. By the big tree to my left. A dark shadow, darker than the forest, which scared me, because how can something be darker than that which is darkest? My fingers clutched the gun. The weight in my hands—the power in my hands—to kill on that perfect morning. The beating in my chest. The power in my hands. It was a perfect morning. I could smell it happening. The flowers would soon stir. The dew would soon glisten. The bread would soon rise. My breathing slowed; I focused. A shadow. An exhale. A noise.

The shadow, it moved. It came toward me. My hands tightened around the gun. I stepped back—I was scared again, for a moment I was scared again, and then I stopped. My father's words were in my ear again, whispering at me to hold steady. To hold still. To listen.

The clink of the lock, and the guard pushes the door open. His hands take my plate, my white plate with the chip. His lips are moving, his eyes are on my plate, my mother's egg-yolk dress. A man in black pushes past him, a book in his hands. His voice rumbles. My mouth is dry, my throat tight.

I sucked in the chilled morning air through clenched teeth. My fear took over; for a second it took over. The shadow moved closer. A rustle, a crack, a cough. The muted light. The beating in my chest loud, too loud. I thought the shadow might hear it. I tried not to panic. We all have to kill sometimes. And what a thing, to kill on a perfect morning.

God forgives you. Words penetrate. I stare at the man priest. His beard moves up and down, his eyes read from his book. The guard shivers by the door. Thirteen steps, thirteen steps, thirteen steps. I want to yell, to scream, to tell them about the dark, the cold, but I can't. My mouth won't open.

I inhaled. I steadied my hands. The rifle cold against my skin. Weak morning light sifted through the leaves. I thought about putting Peter's gun down. Walking away. Running away. Back home to warmth. To laughter. Chores. And emptiness. But the shadow moved, fast, and there he was. A rustle, a cough—a man. Standing in front of me. He looked me in the eye.

The guard's dirty sleeve brushes my hand. He hauls me up; my toast on the floor, crushed. My heart beats against my ribs, my heart hurts. I draw breath in tight gasps. The man in black follows as the guard pulls me along. My last walk, my last morning.

His eyes, blue, looked through me. The weight in my hands, it felt good— powerful. My arms ached but I kept the rifle up. One eye closed. His eyes looking through me. His eyes like my father's eyes.

The courtyard is deserted. Thirteen steps and I'm at the top. The guard shoves me into position as others file into the courtyard. They have faces I don't recognize. I look for my mother in her yellow dress, my sister's toes, Peter in my black coat—I am alone.

He opened his mouth to speak and I pulled the trigger. He was looking me in the eye and then he fell out of the light and into darkness. The shock. My trembling hands dropped the weight of the gun. It was done. What had I done?

The wood creaks under my feet. I shuffle along in the dirt. The guard pulling me, the man in black following. I try to breathe but the silence is suffocating. I turn to look at the man in black but he looks away. No one will look me in the eye.

The light, it was the light. It was too dark, too cold, too blue, too much the same. I was the light. The stillness. It was my father's breath hot on my cheek, his words in my ear. It was hunger pinning me in place. It was. To kill on a perfect morning.

His blue eyes burning into mine. A long drop in the morning air.

The birds had not yet stirred.

SPENT

I wake up depressed, my head spins—hurts, my eyes can't focus—am I high?—I don't think so, I haven't taken drugs in years, but maybe what people said over sputtering candles was right, maybe little molecules, small fragments of nights passed, of drugs consumed, really do keep living on in the tiny spaces of our bodies, hiding like the memories of hurt you'd rather disappear forever, and sometimes, like a clump of flour that has been covered in water but not exposed and dissolved, they become exposed and fluff, like a seeded dandelion head you blow on during summer days, and like those seeds, your hidden past is blown through your blood and you are forced to remember, and then you wake up feeling high, like you just dissolved a little pill against your tongue, but instead of feeling a rush of euphoria you move straight into the bad part, the part where you're tired and you just want to collapse into a bed, your body worn out and used—your love spent.

BE MY FOREVER, FOREVER

When Stacy met Reni, he was just the man behind the counter. The figure in white who prepared her tuna sandwich in thoughtful silence. Then he became the man with whom she held halting conversations about the weather.

Slowly, like a barrel filling with rainwater, she collected details about him. Like the way Reni smiled with half his mouth. And when she said something particularly outrageous—then, and only then, was she granted a full grin.

Or the way he kept his eyes averted and focused on the counter in front of him. Until she began to share her secrets, then he'd put the knife down. Lay the lettuce, bread, and tomatoes on the cutting board, look up, and really listen.

She told him about the time she stole her parents' car without knowing how to drive. How she crashed into a parked van with a baby seat strapped inside it. How, when she peered through one window, she saw the van was filled with trash and broken toys, and how she didn't feel that bad about driving away without leaving a note because if they didn't care about keeping the inside clean, they probably wouldn't care about a few dents.

She told him that her parents never found out about the accident because their car was already busted up from when her mom slid it against the garage wall backing out. Stacy explained to Reni how it felt that night to lie in bed knowing she'd done this thing and no one would ever find out. How her ears strained through the small vibrations of the appliances that filled the house for the wail of a police siren that never came. How soon the whole thing felt made up.

She told him that most of her memories felt made up.

Reni said that if that was the worst thing she'd ever done in her life, then she was a saint.

But that wasn't the worst thing. That was only the first worst thing.

As he passed her a tub of soup, she noticed the way his hand trembled slightly when their skin brushed, and she filed that away in the special Reni file in her brain.

/

The first time Reni saw Stacy outside the deli, he felt like his skin was on inside out, or like he was walking backward in the wrong direction. She hadn't seen him, so—in a moment he didn't even truly register—he began following her. Four paces behind, maybe six. He walked where she walked, his feet spilling over the marks she made in the snow.

She was heading down a grey street in their grey city, her hands clutching mismatched shopping bags blazoned with colourful images. He followed her until the light faded from the sky and there was only darkness left. He followed her until she led him to a park. And then down a path. And then into the woods. He followed her until he lost her in the darkness.

The next day he found a parcel sitting out in front of the deli, his name scrawled across it in halting strokes. The parcel was the kind his grandmother might send him, wrapped in brown butcher paper and a ribbon made of twine. He brought it inside and left it on his desk. He knew it was from her. He didn't know how, but he knew. When he sniffed the paper, it smelled like lemons and lavender, her scent, but also musky, like maybe she had run the paper over her body and into her secret places before wrapping the box.

The thought of her naked and thinking of him, of her rubbing the paper against herself, made him hard. That was the first time he masturbated to Stacy. He imagined himself bending her over the desk and taking her from behind in quick thrusts that made her scream. He imagined muffling her mouth with a towel until he came inside her.

Reni didn't open the package.

/

Stacy waited. She'd reserved the table two days before. It was her and Reni's five-month anniversary, which was the kind of thing she always considered friends stupid for when celebrating, but that she now wanted to celebrate more than anything.

Reni was coming straight from the deli. He'd promised to change. She wore a new-old dress. Pink velvet. Black shiny boots. White stockings. She'd bought each item separately.

Stacy's fingers moved over the flatware, shuffling the knives and forks into straighter rows as she glanced at her watch. Something inside told her this night was going to be spectacular, that they—she and Reni—were spectacular. Her face flushed with the knowledge that everyone else in the restaurant would be watching them with envy.

By the time Reni slipped through the door, the restaurant had quieted into soft whispers. Stacy's grin had faded. The other customers weren't looking at her with envy anymore, just pity. But there he was, shuffling to the table. Training his eyes on the gleaming silver, he handed her a bunch of flowers wrapped in the brown waxed butcher paper she recognized from the deli. Daffodils, wilted. Stacy smiled anyhow, trying to recapture her energy from earlier in the night. She knew owning a deli was a lot of work.

Reni slipped off his jacket and in a smooth motion seated himself opposite her. She could see the place on his sleeve stained by stray mayo, and she felt her smile stiffen. Reni looked up at her and for the first time that evening gave her a smile of his own, quick and timid. Stacy noticed the way his hair was tussled from running his hands through it all day, like he did when the deli was busy. Her body softened. He was always trying.

"How about some champagne?" she suggested.

"If you want."

His voice came out low and soft. Its deep tremor flew through Stacy and she felt a tumultuous pull inside—she felt it whenever Reni was near. Her body responded to his as if an invisible cord lashed them together. Stacy licked her lips and flipped her hair over one shoulder. His deep green eyes looked into hers and she slid a hand across the table to clutch his.

"I do want," she said, smiling.

Reni gave her that half smile she loved before pulling her hand up to his mouth and kissing it. She felt her body becoming aroused like it always did when he touched her. Stacy hadn't had sex with Reni yet. She wanted for them to be together forever. You couldn't do that if you were just fucking.

Stacy remembered the night she'd decided to make it last with Reni. She led him around the city while he was doing his best to follow her without her knowing. She wanted to see how long it would take for him to get bored and stop, but he never did. He sat down in the wooded area in the park she'd led him to—in the snow and dark. And she had felt him sitting there watching her as she stared up at the sky. She was freezing as she sat and waited for him to leave. But he stayed until the dawn bathed him in light and he had to leave to go to work. She knew then that she wouldn't let him fuck her, because she loved him that much already.

⟋

Reni's apartment was filled with new things. Colourful things. Things he'd never even known a person needed.

When he'd asked Stacy to move in, she'd leapt at him. Had pulled him tight against her as she yelled yes before plunging her tongue into his mouth. He remembered that now as he jerked himself off in their shared closet. He didn't want her to know this side of him, the one that thought about her spread-eagled and tied to a bed for him. Stacy was too pure for that. He hadn't even seen her naked yet. But he knew where she was: in the bath, soaking and watching one of her TV shows, a thought that made him moan into the rack of her dresses.

As he was wiping up, Reni got a text from his bread guy, who had to do his delivery that evening because of some family thing. Reni texted back *okay* because that's what happened sometimes.

He popped his head into the bathroom, keeping his eyes averted from her surrounded by bubbles. "I have to meet Joe at the deli," he said.

"Who's Joe?"

"Bread guy," Reni said before ducking back out of the steamy room. He thought he heard her sigh, but he pulled on his jacket anyway, forcing himself not to picture her naked in the tub.

⟋

When Reni rolled over beside her in his sleep, Stacy's body recoiled before moving into the cold spot at the bed's edge. The room they slept in was painted an awful shade of off-white, like the underside of a dead fish. Reni promised he would paint over it as soon as he hired some help at the deli, so but after a year Stacy had given up asking. It would never happen.

And that was Reni. A never-going-to-happen.

Stacy slid quietly out of the sheets, her bare feet hitting the carpeted floor. Reni was a light sleeper, so she crept out of the room on the balls of her feet. Once downstairs, she let herself breathe. A full, deep-in-the-diaphragm breath. The kind of breath she could never take in their bedroom.

She couldn't see the man who filled her mind with mystery anymore. Now he was just a lump of silence, content to work and to sleep. Stacy had considered having sex with him, even though the fire that used to run through her whenever he touched her had extinguished, because maybe if he wasn't her forever-forever, he could at least be her right-now, until forever actually showed up. She could have sex with a right-now.

/

Reni hovered over her face, his smile contained. He pushed back her hair before whispering, "I'll be back late, love. There's coffee and breakfast in the oven."

Stacy let her eyes roam his face. He had forgotten a small patch of hair on his cheek when shaving. Her fingertips brushed over this mistake, and she felt a familiar flare in her belly. She pulled his face down to hers, pushing her lips against his, spilling her passion into him.

He pulled away after a few moments.

"Don't go," Stacy whispered. "Let the shop stay closed, just for one day, let people imagine you're off on an adventure." She pictured them together and started to feel wetness between her legs.

"You know I can't do that, love." Reni straightened before pulling his hands away from her bare thigh.

Stacy felt the heat fade as she pulled her arms back around her body. She rolled to the side, letting her frustration pool under the couch cushions. She listened to Reni leave. The lock flipped. The door closed. And she was alone. Again.

/

Reni fought against her anger with silence and by retreating into the only space still his own—the deli. He didn't know how to make her happy anymore. He still dreamed of her, but his mind had also begun to wander. He rarely masturbated to her anymore and when he did, it was unremarkable, with none of the urgency from before.

/

Stacy was sitting at the kitchen table eating alone again. Since she'd first thought about leaving Reni, a year and a half ago, they'd had sex only once. He had pushed into her, but it hadn't been what she thought it was going to be. It was too fast and too slow all at the same time, and afterward she was glad he wasn't her forever-forever person.

The next day, she'd loaded her stuff into a truck and then headed to her sister's. Stacy even packed away her memory of Reni sitting alone in the woods, buried it until it didn't feel real. Like her whole life had never felt real.

/

Reni sat alone in the bathtub. It was empty, but he could still see the glitter from Stacy's bath bubbles. In his lap he held the parcel she'd left him outside the deli. The writing had faded. He lifted it to his nose but he couldn't smell her anymore.

She'd really left.

He lay back and drummed his fingers against the box, before getting up and dropping it into the trash. With that final action, Reni left Stacy too.

✦

Stacy felt Danny's hand squeeze hers. He was laughing into his phone. She tried to focus on the pavement. Tried to track the boot treads in the snow. Tried not to look up and see the deli.

But she did look up.

The street was its usual lazy tunnel; people sauntered by, going from the produce shop to the fish market to the bakery, filling bags with treats for the weekend.

Danny stopped midstride and let go of her hand. He shifted his phone from one ear to the other as he rummaged around his bag for something.

She drifted away. One step and then another. Closer to the deli.

It looked cold. The lights were off, she realized. There was a piece of butcher paper taped to the door. She could tell it was Reni's handwriting, but she couldn't make out the words. Stacy looked back at Danny. He was absorbed in writing something down, so she walked the small distance to stand in front of the shop. Her heart fluttered.

Reni's scrawled handwriting. She lifted a hand to the glass. Tried to feel him there, tried to feel his familiar tug in the deepest part of her. Deli for sale. Call the number for details. And that was it.

He lived in the small details. The way the *D* flourished beside a cramped *e*. His hesitation on the *s* in sale.

Stacy felt her throat constrict. She cupped a hand on the glass and peered into the darkness. Everything was the same as the first day she'd ordered a tuna melt. The same as when she danced inside with Reni late after closing. When she'd told him about the time she jumped from a bridge and thought, for a second, that she might die, and that would be okay. She closed her eyes and thought she could hear the hum of the fridges through the glass.

A hand gripped her shoulder. She smiled and almost exclaimed, "Reni," but when she turned it was to Danny's grinning face instead.

"You hungry? I saw a place a few blocks back that looked amazing. I'd be up for some food." Danny leaned down and kissed her neck. She felt herself warm. She brought her hand away from the glass, and the hum faded.

COME AND GET YOUR ICE CREAM, MOTHERFUCKERS

He heard the music before he was fully awake. The notes descending onto his consciousness like feathers falling out of a cloudy dark sky.

BA dum BA dum BA dum BA da da BA da da DAAA dum.

He groaned. Even during that light tendril of awake time—as soon as he opened his eyes, even the barest of a crack—he felt it. The throbbing in the back of his skull. A distant pain kept at bay only by the emptying of consciousness at night. By midday it would be a drill in his temples. By evening, a lasso tightening its grip around the entire circumference of his head.

BA dum BA dum BA dum BA da da BA da da DAAA dum.

The notes: they squirmed in him, they pushed their way into the tiny spaces between cells. He imagined them clinging to the discs of hemoglobin running through his veins, rocketing the up-down-up-down tune through the entirety of his body until even his toes—no, even his toenails—were alive with the looping scratches of sound.

BA dum BA dum BA dum BA da da BA da da DAAA dum.

But at least he still had his dreams, or, rather, the absence of them, to offer escape. That period between midnight and mid-morning when he slept blissfully unaware in his twin bed. He tried to keep the distance between the awake him and the sleeping him as long as possible.

BA dum BA dum BA dum BA da da BA da da DAAA dum.
The garbage can beside his night table a testament: the rumpled packaging, the bold red letters, punching him in the face; SLEEP NOW, SLEEP FOREVER, SLEEP IS BETTER THAN BEING ALIVE, SLEEP IS THE DARKNESS OF CALM. He shovelled a handful into his mouth every night before stretching out on his back and falling into the rabbit hole. He hated them. But he needed them. So he loved them too.

BA dum BA dum BA dum.
He swivelled his body up and out of bed.

BA da da BA da da da da DAA dum.
His feet fumbled till they found his slippers, worn things they were, given to him years ago for Christmas when his mother was still alive to give presents. He slowly shuffled in time with the notes ringing in his ears.

BA dum BA dum BA dum BA da da BA da da DAAA dum.
His eyes bored into the mirror, searching for a hint of the rhythm there. For a beat, maybe two, he thought he saw it lurking in the corner of the left. A thick black smudge. He shifted his focus to the flesh surrounding his eye. Sallow skin, dusty and tight, wrinkles that stretched from the creases to his hairline in downward strokes. He smiled—tried to, at least—but instead of looking like a kindly ice cream man, he resembled a grimacing spectre. His smile twitched as the pain in his temples flared, and he dropped the corners of his mouth to cover his yellow teeth.

BA dum BA dum BA dum BA da da BA da da da da DAA dum DA da du da da da dum DA da du da da da dum DA da du da da da da dum Da da DUM.

He fumbled his keys. The monstrous whiteness of his truck overtook the sun and cast him in shadow. His nerves vibrated with the overworked tune.

BA dum BA dum BA dum.

He finally got the door open, and his body settled into the bouncy driver's seat, but for long moments that overlapped, he couldn't bring himself to turn the engine on. Because once he did, it would only be a few moments more before he had to hit the road, and hitting the road meant driving, and driving meant turning on the music, and that meant more pain.

BA da da BA da da da da DAA dum.

But he had to. His whole life, his livelihood, every scrap of a cent he had managed to eke out in his nearly sixty years was because of the damnable truck, with its hideous colours and sugar wrapped in ice wrapped in a polluting package. Every moment of his existence was woven into the fibre of the vehicle he sat in. It gave him life even as it took it away.

Their faces turned up in gleeful anticipation, their eyes overcome with such powerful emotion that tears threatened to leak from the corners and splash their bare chests with salty water, mingling with the sweat from the burning summer sun. They'd run him down, bare feet slapping against the hot asphalt as he drove forward, the speaker reverberating so hard his teeth shook.

BA dum BA dum BA dum.

He made them bang their tiny fists against the back bumper before slowing to a complete halt; they had to really want it, they had to prove themselves. They needed something to boast to their dads about over barbecued chicken and pickle-juice potato salad. Later in life they would remember, he liked to imagine, the moment they'd chased the ice cream man until their feet bleed, until their lungs burned, until they thought he would never stop. But then he did—because they hadn't given up. Because they were heroes.

BA dum BA dum BA dum BA da da BA da da DAAA dum.

They handed their sweaty-fisted sheets of money and piles of coins up to him. He handed them ice cream that ran down their forearms, soaking them in sugar and summer. chocolate, vanilla, lemon, lavender, tigggger, pink, green, ones that sparkled, ones that tasted so good you could melt into them instead of the other way around, others that had been sitting in his truck too long, always overlooked.

And with every shriek of joy, with every burble of speech, his eye twitched, his jaw locked, his head pounded. With every stumble of a simple request for th-th-th-thhhat one, for every this one no that one no this one no that one, for every *BA dum BA dum BA dum BA da da BA da da da da DAA dum*, his vision narrowed. His heart beat tighter. He felt his rage, yes, his rage—he felt it in the tips of his fingers, in every strand of hair on his head. He felt it in his dilated pupils, in his intestines twisting around and around and around, he was filled to the brim with *DA da du da da da dum DA da du da da da dum DA da du da da da du dum Da da DUM.*

But this time: this time, his eyes came to rest above the tops of the kids' heads—above their babbling, above their high-pitched squeals, on a piece of silver glinting in the strong noon sun. A *put down for a moment to take a break and have a smoke* saviour.

He left his truck to idle in the heat, the kids satisfied and running in circles. But not the song. It drifted alongside him, inside him, outside him—weaving into his rage. He took mammoth steps, his stride gulping the pavement. The silver glint glinted as he drew closer, until it was in his hand.

BA dum BA dum BA dum BA da da BA da da da da—
In a movement quicker than a *BA dum* he had the drill against his temple, and then the drill inside his head, the drill inside his brain.
BA dum—
It wouldn't stop.
Ba dum—
IT WOULDN'T STOP.
BA dum—
Kids screamed.
BA da da—
Blood soaked the left collar of his white coveralls.
BA da da da da—
He put the drill down. He couldn't see properly.
DΛΛ dum—
The kids kept shrieking as he staggered back to his truck.
DA da du da da da dum—
He wrenched the door open and with slippery hands, hauled his body inside by gripping the wheel, then set his foot like a lead weight onto the gas.
DA da du da da da dum—
His left eye twitched like mad, blackness-then-light, blackness-then-light, his truck listed to the side, his head listed to the side. The hole in his head leaking.
DA da du da da da dum—
He slowed the truck just before the bend in the road, where it curled around an oceanside cliff. The notes filled him, they filled the air inside the truck, the slivered cracks in the pails that held the ice cream, the microscopic air bubbles trapped inside the creamy mucus, the permafrost.
Da da DUM—
He jumped free as the truck flew off the cliff.

✦

The gravel of the road poked into the soft flesh between his shoulder blades. The sun burned into his eyes, a perfect blaze of white. Pain crept back in, as if it had only left to get a drink before sulking back into his broken body. He could hear one bird, a shrill melody that echoed off the trees.

He could hear one bird.

Only one bird.

MAIL

You're a worthless selfish fucking shit of a human being who can't even do one thing right.

I hate you.

You should splash—no, belly flop—into the most freezing water that exists on this planet, where even the penguins and fattest of whales can't live. You should go drown yourself with the shock of how horrible you are.

You can't even create properly.

You can't even write a fucking sentence without it coming out bland as boiled potatoes. You are boiled potatoes. No one cares what worthless things you put on the page. But you keep writing because that's how terrible a person you are.

You never get the message.

Fuck.

If you do one good thing in your entire life, do this: Listen to me. I'm not trying to be mean. I just can't contain it anymore. Just quit and save us all. Save yourself.

Bye.

I love you.

LAST

It happened one night, I'm not sure how long ago. It's hard to keep track of time now.

I was alone, as usual, watching a movie about a quirky, awkward girl and a clumsy, handsome man. They were just about to kiss under twinkling lights in a flower garden. It was a clichéd scene, the kind where they look earnestly into each other's eyes, willing each other to lean in first. With my arms wrapped around my pillow and tears streaming down my face, I chanted words of encouragement.

And as their lips were about to meet, it happened. Darkness. The power clicked off and then I was alone, really, really alone. Though I wouldn't know just how alone until later.

I did all of the things a person is supposed to do in the event of a power outage. I crept between my ground-level apartment's rooms with the light of a small lavender-scented candle. When I reached the breaker box, I noticed all the switches were still in the on position, which was weird because there was no power at all. I went to my kitchen window and peered out. All the street lamps were off and none of the neighbours' houses shone with light. When I stepped outside to see if any of my neighbours were as confused as I was, I noticed—for the first time since moving from the prairies to Vancouver—that I could see the stars. Not just the super bright ones and the moving satellite ones—I mean all of them. There was no orange glow from the city lights. There was also no sound. No one else panicking. No one else anything.

I looked at my watch and realized it had stopped ticking. Maybe it was later than I thought and everyone was asleep.

Since there was nothing I could do, I walked back inside and into my bedroom. I turned the TV off—it would wake me up when the power did come back on—then took a couple sleeping pills. I blew out my candle. And then I slept for a long time.

❧

When I woke the next day, it was already dusk. The food in my fridge was all sloppy and warm, so I poured a bowl of cereal and ate it dry. As I chewed, I looked out at my street. I couldn't hear the screaming baby from next door. I wanted to feel something, panic maybe, but I just felt nothing.

Maybe the sleeping pills had made me groggy.

After I ate, I remembered I had to feed Gordie, the fighting fish with the rainbow tail I'd bought at my counsellor's advice. But he was dead. I ladled him out of the bowl and took him to the kitchen. The matchbox I'd used the previous evening was still sitting open on the counter. I shook the rest of the matches out and placed Gordie inside.

By then it was starting to get dark, so I went back to my room and lit another candle, grabbed a book, and began to read. I promised to bury Gordie later.

❧

When I finished my book, the sun was all the way up. I left my room and peered out again at the street. Nothing. My electronics still weren't working, my lights were still off, and I still hadn't seen another person. I'd been listening for my neighbours from upstairs to thump around or, you know, make any noise at all, but nothing. They hadn't come to the door asking about the breaker box either, which was weird but okay too because I didn't like them anyway.

I had a crank radio under the sink, but when I cranked it, nothing came out. Flicking my TV, laptop, and regular radio on and off did nothing. I decided I needed call my sister. I only have one. She still lives on the prairies with our parents but she always watched the news, or would have seen something on Facebook about what was happening. Also, her number was the only one in my phone.

My phone wouldn't turn on. Shaking it didn't work, slamming it against the counter didn't work. All right. I didn't panic. I was okay, I didn't really need to call anyone. I was sure the city would figure everything out. Until then, I estimated I had enough water and canned food to last seventy-two hours, the number they say you always need. I could live another day without a shower.

I ate a can of cold soup at my kitchen table and settled in to wait for things to turn on. When they didn't, I went back to bed and took another couple sleeping pills. I'm sure my counsellor wouldn't agree with the amount of sleeping pills I was taking, but whatever. She would never know.

❧

Hunger drove me out of the house days later. All my boxes of cereal and my canned goods were in the recycle bin, and my cupboards were bare. I knew it was time to leave to get supplies.

I didn't want to go to the Safeway. I was sure there'd be too many people and that they'd be panicking. I mean, I'd seen the news when other cities lost power. It was always the same. The corner store on the next block, that would be the easier option. I knew they jacked up their prices but I didn't really care. I collected all my emergency cash from the book on the shelf where I kept it in a secret hole carved into the pages.

Outside, the quiet was ominous. There were no birds, no insects, no humans—still nothing. And it was hot, like fucking desert hot. I'd noticed the heat inside, kind of, but living in a ground level meant I was mostly cool and damp. Plus I kept my blinds closed, except for when I was expressly looking through them. So the heat was a shock.

I pulled off my hoodie and meandered down the street. Cars were lined up as perfectly as any other day. The only difference was the lack of people. I don't usually notice people anyway, but not having anyone around gave me goose bumps: it was just creepy. As I got to the corner of my block, I started to look for signs of people—of first responders or police, of anybody, really—even a single cat would have been awesome. My neighbourhood was filled with cats roaming the streets. I usually couldn't walk a block without being glared at by one, watching me from a porch.

✎

The corner store's door was open a crack. It was dark inside, and my reflection was visible on the door in the afternoon light. I looked myself over and winced. It was bad. I'd thrown my matted hair in a quick bun on top of my head, my jeans were crumpled, and I was sweating through my T-shirt.

I pushed the door open all the way and took a hesitant step inside.

"Hello?" My voice echoed. "Hey, anybody here?"

Okay, so at this point I started to get a little worried. Nadi, the owner, was always here. Eight in the morning till eleven at night, he never took a day off.

Through the darkness I could see rows and rows of food. Food so filled with preservatives it would last well after the power eventually came back on. I liked Nadi; I didn't want to steal from him. But I was hungry. Then I remembered that paper and pens existed. A note with cash left on the counter would be fine. I grabbed a bag from behind the till and walked to the rows of food, examining everything there was to offer. In the end I filled the bag with soup, crackers, chips, and candy.

Back on the street I noticed how tired I still was. I'd just woken up, but I was already ready to go back to bed. It might have been the heat, it might have been the sleeping pills. All I knew was that outside was creeping me the fuck out and I wanted to be back in my house.

✦

I was starting to smell. It had been four days since the power went out, and the water wasn't running so I hadn't showered. My skin was sticky with the heat and my hair was oily. I'd been drinking water from an old flat of bottles I kept in the back of a closet, but I was almost out.

✦

By now, I realized I should have tried to get to work. I'd already missed two shifts. But I hated my job at the liquor store so I decided, fuck it. If they wanted to fire me because of this power outage, let them. I'd only been working there a few weeks anyhow.

I'd never held down a job for much longer than that. It was the calling in sick all the time, I knew it was, but I just hated to go outside. And people. People fucking suck—or rather, sucked. Or maybe I was the one who sucked.

✒

On day seven, I realized that I really was all alone.

When I woke up that morning—or afternoon, I couldn't tell which—I felt the urge to see someone. To know when the power would come back on.

I walked from house to house, knocked on door after door. No one answered. No dogs barked. I peered in windows, but all the houses were empty. When I reached Broadway Street, I saw a bus sitting in the middle of the intersection. Farther down, two cars had smashed together, but they weren't totally destroyed. It looked like they had just coasted into each other. The farther down Broadway I walked, the more car accidents I saw—but they were the only evidence something major had happened.

I didn't find a human body in those early days, and I've never found one since. I was the only human still in existence.

There was no debris or anything indicating fire or any other emergency. When I walked past Safeway, I retched from the smell. The heat had sped up the decomposition of the fresh food and meat. That's what I remember most from those first few weeks, the smell of rotting food floating around everywhere.

After that day, I mostly stuck close to home. It was too uncomfortable to go any farther.

✒

When I finally gathered the nerve to walk the few blocks down to the ocean, dead fish were piled up on the shoreline, their puffy bodies moving in rhythm with the tides. The smell made me gag, so I walked back home and didn't leave for another two days.

✦

Time is broken up into awake time and sleep time. Day time and night time. Eating time and not eating time. Reading time and exploring time.

Time is nothing. I didn't understand that until this happened.

✦

I'd spent so much of my adult life alone—in my room reading books or watching TV—that, I guess, for a long time, being the only person left on Earth was okay. But after I'd read all my books, I started to think. And then I started to get scared.

More than that, I started to wish for the parties and the experiences I'd never had.

✦

The first house I went into belonged to the normally intrusive neighbour lady across the street. It was still scorching outside during the day, but I was becoming accustomed to the heat.

Before I went, I'd been lying on my living room floor trying to see pictures in the ceiling. It occurred to me that I didn't have anything nice to wear in the heat. All I had were thick jeans and sweat-baked T-shirts. Then I remembered how my neighbour wore bright flowing clothes, like chiffon and silk. I figured I could dare to experiment.

Her house was crammed full from floor to ceiling. Every square inch was filled with stuff, except for a small path that I had to turn sideways to shuffle through. Everything you could imagine was in that house. Newspapers from twenty years ago, multiple copies of the same issues. A room filled with bins of crafting supplies. The kitchen had garbage everywhere.

When I found the bedroom—a room with a single cot and a full-length mirror—it seemed to hold every piece of clothing ever invented. I picked my way through the mess until I found the dress I was looking for. She had showed it to me once, offered to give it to me, but I'd refused—it was too nice then, too pretty for me. I pulled off my clothes and pulled it on. I was beautiful. I'd never thought of myself as beautiful before, but now, with no one to compare myself to, I realized I was beautiful.

I walked out of my neighbour's house and into the sun. Halfway across the street, I started to cry.

/

It's amazing what you can do when you have nothing to do. I uncovered some art supplies in a split-level house. The guy who'd lived there liked painting nude women with dog heads. I took one for my living room. I'd never painted in my life, so I started with a mural on the outside of my house. Blue flowers, dancing trees, little cats and dogs scampering. It was fun.

/

When the food was gone from the corner store, I started to steal from the houses. Everyone had at least one cupboard filled with canned Campbell's soup and apple juice. I also took other things, like a bag of weed from my upstairs neighbours, and a gold bracelet from a red house with a big truck parked out front.

/

The weather didn't change. The seasons didn't change. I didn't keep track of time, of the days and months. I just knew it felt like it'd been summer forever.

/

I started to find the shrivelled bodies of bugs hidden in dark corners of the places I visited. Massive amounts of them, piled up in heaps. I found so many I stopped looking.

/

There was a stretch where all I did was lie in bed and look at pictures of my family. I tried to remember why I'd felt like I needed to move far away from them to be happy, why we'd fought so much, but I couldn't. All I could remember was snuggling on the couch, swimming at the lake in the summer, bursts of laughter from my sister over the phone.

I'd tried, for the first few months, to figure out what had happened. But I couldn't; I was just a regular girl. I never graduated high school. I didn't have any friends. I needed to see, or rather had needed to see, a shrink to help me be able to leave the house. I'm no one special. I still don't know where everyone went, and I don't know why I didn't go with them.

Some days, I miss everyone. Other days, I'm just really glad to be alone.

/

There will be no one to read this, but I feel like I have to write something, so: goodbye, I guess. It seems kinda sad that I was the only one to survive and that soon I'm going to be gone. I'm sure humanity would have liked a better survivor, someone who could have been a champion. But, well, I'm just too lonely, I guess. Or maybe I'm just too tired. Or maybe nothing. Fuck it. I just want to get out of this heat.

/

Stephanie put the pen and paper down on the brown lawn. She figured this was as good a place to die as any other. There would be no one to find her body, and no animals to eat it, so why not here? She was wearing the beautiful dress she'd taken from her neighbour, a necklace she'd found in an old lady's house, and perfume that smelled like lavender. She was ready. She held the orange bottle up to her face and squinted at the label one more time before tipping the pills into her mouth.

Just as she was about to swallow, there was a bang from the other side of the street. She whipped her head up, her mouth bulging with pills, and caught a flash of white over by the car she'd painted into a rabbit. The pills were dissolving in her mouth and tasted horrible.

A head popped up from behind the rabbit-car and she almost choked. It was a guy: black hair, scruffy beard, and a huge smile. He leapt, laughing. "Oh my fucking God. Oh. My. Fucking. God," he said as he bounced up and down.

Stephanie breathed heavily out of her nose, her heart pounding.

The guy ran over and fell on her lawn, still laughing. "Oh my fucking God. You're a you," he said.

Stephanie leaned back from him but kept her eyes on his face as he rolled around the grass. Saliva was starting to drip down her chin.

"I'm, ah, Mark, oh my fucking God. You're alive, right? I'm not going crazy?"

Stephanie shook her head no.

"What's wrong with you? Your mouth? I'm like so, oh my God, you know you're the only person I've seen, right?"

Stephanie watched him. All she felt was fear, and an uncomfortable realization about how ugly she looked sitting there in her breezy dress. Her skin crawled like it used to when she was around strangers. He held out his hand to her. She flinched, felt her eyes wide with uncertainty, while his beamed with happiness. She grabbed her water bottle. It didn't matter that he was here and if he really was here and she was still alone. And she liked it that way, even if she didn't.

She swallowed the pills.

"What was that?" he asked.

Stephanie tucked the pill bottle behind her.

He looked at her house. "I like your mural."

"Thanks."

"Who are you?" he asked.

"Stephanie."

"I'm Mark. I already said that but yeah, I'm Mark."

"What's happening?" Stephanie asked.

"I don't know," he said. "I just woke up one day and it was like this."

"I was watching a movie."

"Oh, which one?"

"Nothing special."

"I like your dress, Stephanie."

"Thanks."

Stephanie stared at Mark as he looked around at her neighbourhood.

"You got any food?" he asked.

"Uh, yeah, in the kitchen. Some cans of soup."

"Awesome, I love soup."

"Where did you come from?" she asked.

"Me, oh, I, uh, walked here, I guess."

"From where?"

"Well, up the coast, I don't really know where I was, but it was up the coast."

"How do you not know where you came from?"

"Oh, I uh—I was, am—a traveller of sorts."

"A traveller?"

"Yeah, I sort of just hitchhiked around wherever other people were going."

"That's weird. Didn't you, like, miss having a house?"

"Nah, I liked it. I still like it. Although now I've been walking everywhere for a long time."

"You've been walking this whole time?"

"Yeah, it's empty out there."

"So there's really no one?"

"Nope, just you and me, I guess."

Stephanie's stomach cramped and she felt a wave of dizziness. She began to see double; she closed her eyes. The pills were starting to come back up, so she forced them back down again with a chug from her water bottle.

"Hey, are you okay?"

"I'm fine, just hot."

"Let's go inside then."

"No."

"Hey, I'm not some like perv or something. You don't have to worry."

"I'm not worried about that."

"You're not?"

"No."

"Thanks. But really, if you're too hot we should go inside, or at least sit in the shade."

The pill bottle dug into her hip. "No, really, I'm okay."

The breeze picked up and the corners of Stephanie's papers fluttered up. Mark went to grab them, but she stopped him.

"Don't."

"What are you writing?"

"It's nothing."

"Can I read it?"

Stephanie felt so heavy. She lay down on her side. "Not till after."

"After what?"

"After...dinner."

"Oh, okay."

She couldn't keep her eyes open anymore.

"Are you sure you're okay? You don't look okay."

"Yeah, I'm fine."

Stephanie felt a hot breeze on her face. The grass tickled her toes. She closed her eyes as she listened to Mark.

"Well, I don't know if you realized this yet or not, but there are dead fish everywhere. It used to stink really bad, and now there's just creepy bones along the shorelines. But at the same time, everything is beautiful now. Because nothing's the same. It's all become so slow and natural. I miss animals, though. And bugs, even though I hate bugs."

Stephanie gave him a quiet hmmm as she drifted further and further away.

"And well, let's see, I'm really glad I found you because, honestly, I was starting to go a little fucking aghhh. I kept thinking, like, why? Why was I the only one left? Me. I haven't done anything important or anything. And then I thought that maybe actually I was the only one who died, and that this was my hell, or heaven even, I guess. But then here you are, so now I don't know."

Stephanie could barely hear Mark anymore.

"Are we the only ones? Maybe there are more? Right? I mean, it can't just be us?"

Mark went on talking to her about things he'd seen walking, about piles of bugs in the forest and piles of cars on the highways and how strange downtowns felt when they were empty. Eventually, he put a hand on her shoulder to wake her up. He was hungry.

She didn't move.

He shook her shoulder.

She still didn't move.

"Uh, hello, Stephanie? Are you okay?"

He shook her again.

"Um, don't get sick or anything because, like, there's no doctors anymore."

Mark touched her face, then her neck. He felt for her pulse. Nothing.

"Stephanie, what the fuck?"

And then he noticed the pill bottle behind her. He picked it up. Seconal. He didn't know what that was. Stephanie looked peaceful, though, he thought, or maybe she was just sleeping. How was he supposed to know?

He gathered the papers she'd told him he couldn't read and moved over to the shade with them. He would only read them until she woke up. Then they would go have dinner and talk about how everything was different, and how they were special, and how they had found each other, and how they weren't alone anymore.

PORNORAMA

Crimson Smithe is creeped out by the mannequin torsos that hang near the store's ceiling, floating above the racks and counters. Their thin, legless, headless bodies, draped in lace and silk, showcase the only parts of a woman's body men apparently need. She takes one of the mannequins down, lays it out on the counter, and blows a layer of dust off its bare shoulders.

Fitting the new lingerie onto the busts is her favourite part of working at the Pornorama. Every third Sunday the new outfits are delivered, wrapped in plastic and boxed in cardboard. She spends the entire graveyard shift slicing each box open, pulling the outfits out one by one, ripping the plastic off, and revelling in the sparkle, glitter, and ribbons that adorn the bras and panties. She lines the lingerie up on the counter, mixing and matching every piece until she's perfected outfits that will lure the strippers from next door to come in and buy them.

The women descend on the shop around three each morning and use their freshly earned loonies and toonies to purchase something new, a trifle they hope will make them enough money to eventually leave this hellhole. Sometimes it even works. Crimson will sell a customer a black thong and never see her again. She imagines those women out on the road, slipping farther and farther away from this horrible town. Dancing until they reach their final destination: a place where they can discard the frills and lace and be different. Better.

Crimson likes that people find her displays enticing enough to return, a lot of the time wearing what they purchased last time. Most of her regulars are rig pigs with too much money to spend and not enough of anything to spend it on. But the strippers lend an air of freshness to the store—they make the clothes more beautiful.

/

Crimson stands in front of the mirror by the counter. She holds a frilly white-and-baby-blue teddy up to her body and sighs.

"Hey, I'll buy that for you," says a man with a wheezy voice.

She grimaces before turning around. It's one of the regulars, Tanner. He rents a movie every night he's off-site. She has to phone him every day to remind him to return his favourites, but like almost everyone in this town, except her, he has way too much money and doesn't care about fines.

She points at the movie he's clutching. "Will that be all?"

He smiles, his lips parting to reveal brown teeth. She fights the urge to retch.

"Come on, girl. Try it on for me, just once."

Crimson drops the teddy and moves behind the counter. She goes to the till and waits for him, her finger grazing the hidden emergency button. Once, she had to press it when she caught a customer masturbating in a corner. By the time the police arrived, the man had cum all over the wall and fled. Crimson left it for the day person to clean up. Ten dollars an hour wasn't enough for her to deal with that shit.

Tanner walks to the till. He puts the movie down and leans in. "I won't tell anyone," he says, pulling a wad of bills from his pocket.

Crimson stares at the money. She hasn't eaten all day. Her rent's been due for weeks and her landlord had cornered her that afternoon and taken all her cash. She leans back and stares into his unfocused eyes. "Fuck off, okay? If you want to see tits, go next door."

"But I've seen all those girls."

"Then fucking go get a chick loaded at Cowboys and pay her to take off her shirt."

He opens his mouth, growling with laughter. The stink of his breath hits Crimson in the face.

She grabs his movie and steps back, then glances down to check the title. *Ass Grabbers Two: Double the Trouble*, she reads, rolling her eyes. She ducks down and opens the drawer that holds all the DVDs. She can feel him watching her as she digs out his DVD from the pile in the drawer. This is why she always wears baggy clothes at work. Her boss demands that she wear some of the tamer outfits for sale, but she always refuses. He doesn't work alone at night like she does.

Finding the DVD, she stands up and shoves it into the case. Tanner is still waving the money in small circles. She stuffs the movie into a thick black bag and tosses it at him. "Ten ninety-nine, due back tomorrow."

He laughs and slams a twenty on the counter. "Keep the change." He winks and staggers out of the store.

Crimson pockets the change. Normally she would insist he take it back, but she's starving. She'll run to the Macs across the street after she's finished with the displays, but before the strippers drop in, and grab some pop and Hot Pockets. The guy who works graveyard there always throws in a bag of chips when she stops in to buy dinner—she assumes it's in solidarity with a fellow night worker. She would do the same for him but he never ventures into her store, at least not during her shift.

✒

Crimson settles onto the stool behind the counter. Behind her, a screen flashes porn. She's begged her boss to get rid of the TV, but he says it drives sales. She once responded that if someone made it that far into the store they were already going to buy something. He laughed and walked back to his office, slamming the door. Crimson knows when to pick her battles, so she let it go. All she has to do is not look behind her. The volume is low, so all that's audible is soft moaning. She can live with soft moaning.

／

Crimson rips into the Hot Pocket. The thick cheese and ham burn her mouth, so she takes a swig of cold Coke. She grabs her sketchbook and a pencil and flips the book open, starts to draw a face. The night before, she'd dreamed of a man with brown hair and green eyes. She'd reached out to trace the stubble on his chin with her fingers, but her hand bumped into the sweaty wall of her trailer. Dark reality. She awoke alone in her single bed, trapped in a town that devours people. But now, at work, she reaches into her memory and draws line after line to capture that fleeting hope, that dream, of someone to love, someone to be with.

／

Country music floats through the store, blending with the soft moaning from the screen behind her. She ignores the throbbing rock and dance music from next door and settles into stillness. She forgets the porn and dildos that need shelving and focuses all of her attention on drawing.

／

The door opens, letting in a rush of hot air. Crimson looks up from her sketchbook. A woman painted to look sexy surveys the store. She smells like lemons, and her hair is held in a huge hairspray poof on top of her head. Damp tendrils stick to the side of her face.

"Hey," Crimson says.

"I hear this is the best place in town to get clothes," the woman rasps.

Crimson sets her sketchbook on the counter. "Depends what you mean by clothes."

The woman laughs, then starts to cough. She beats on her chest before speaking again. "Something to wear to work, to make all the little boys part with their money."

"You work next door?"

"Got in this afternoon. Just finished my first shift."

"I'm Crimson."

"Michelle, or—I guess—Candy, if we're being formal."

Crimson blushes. People always think her name is fake, but her mom had just been really stoned when she'd filled in the birth certificate.

"Can I smoke in here?" Michelle asks.

Crimson glances at the security camera pointed at the till, nods, and drags her stool to the side of the long counter. Her boss was too cheap to install more than one camera and she knows the boundaries of its sight.

Michelle follows Crimson's gaze and smiles as she walks to the end of the counter. She hops up and faces Crimson, shimmying back until she can cross her legs. She digs into her oversized purse and pulls out a squished pack of cigarettes. "You got a light?"

"Behind you."

When Michelle swivels around, her legs uncross, giving Crimson a view of tiny hot-pink panties.

"Dick lights. Haven't seen these before," Michelle says, flicking the lighter on. Fire shoots up through the top of the cock and she wheezes out a laugh.

"People buy them for stagettes," Crimson says.

"Can you imagine pulling this out at a bus stop? Excuse me while I light my cigarette with a dick." Michelle laughs at her own joke. The rawness in her lungs makes Crimson wince. Michelle holds out her squished pack of cigarettes. "Want one?"

"No, I don't smoke."

Michelle shrugs before taking a long draw. Crimson grabs the empty Coke can and hands it over. Michelle flicks the ash into it before leaning back against the top of the counter. Her legs are still open.

"So, whattaya do when you're not working at the Pornorama, Crimson?"

"I like to walk around town, read, sketch. Just usual stuff."

"You got a boyfriend? Girlfriend?"

"No, my ex was a bastard."

"Gotcha. What'd he do? Fuck another pussy?"

Crimson blushes. "And moved out, leaving me with high rent and a shitty apartment."

"Aren't all the places here shitty?"

"Yeah, I guess."

"You from around here?" Michelle takes another long draw from the cigarette. She holds the smoke in her lungs before it starts to escape through her nose.

"No, I moved from Edmonton with him when he got a job up at site. I thought we'd be together forever and all that shit, but now I'm stuck here, renting a room in a trailer barely big enough for me to stand in."

"Why don't you leave?"

"Too broke."

"You could dance. You have nice tits."

Crimson crosses her arms over her chest and stares at Michelle's legs. The skin around her knees is wrinkled, and a bead of sweat trickles down her calf.

"No, I wouldn't be any good at that."

"Sure you would, you just"—Michelle drops her cigarette into the can and jumps off the counter—"shimmy, bend over, and wiggle your ass. Then, just get naked and spin around the pole a few times. But the real money-maker is when you sit on your blanket. You ever seen that? I do a good one. I had all these posters made up, real classy and shit, you know? I had a professional take the pictures, I'm in a red thong, like that one"—Michelle points to a mannequin behind Crimson—"and it's all smoky and the lights are dimmed. Anyway, guys love it. So the blanket, I sit on the edge of the stage, open my legs, and I make a show of rolling up the poster. Then I shove it up my pussy. The guys take turns trying to toss money in. If it goes in they get the poster. Trust me, it makes me loads of cash, and the guys love it because of the smell. They like to think they're getting a piece of you." Michelle hops back on the stool. "Anyway, you could do it, I bet. Once I saw one girl do the same thing but in her ass."

Crimson could never do that.

Michelle lights up another cigarette. "You mind if I keep this?" she says before she tosses the lighter in her purse. "It's too funny."

Crimson shrinks back, and as she does, Michelle notices the sketchbook open beside her. She extends her whole body to reach it.

"What's this?"

"Nothing—just something to pass the time, I guess."

"Who is this guy?"

"I don't know. Just someone from a dream."

"He's hot," Michelle says.

"I guess."

"Wow, fuck, these are good, girl. Why aren't you in school or something?"

Crimson shrugs. "It's too much money."

Michelle keeps flipping through the book.

The door opens again. Both women turn to look.

A young guy stands at the entrance wearing a white T-shirt and jeans. His hair is slicked back and hangs to his shoulders.

"Welcome to the Pornorama," Michelle says, "where all your dreams come true."

The guy smiles and walks toward them. His feet catch on the dirty carpet, and he falls against the far end of the counter.

"Whoa, buddy, you been out having fun tonight?" Michelle asks.

"Only a bit," he says with a smile.

Crimson can feel her face flushing. Unlike most of the regulars, this guy is young and good-looking. Young guys usually get their porn from the internet.

"Do you need any help?" Crimson asks.

"Maybe," he says, looking at her with a shy smile.

"Okay."

He looks around. "I'm, uh, looking for something. As a gift."

Crimson suppresses a smile. She's heard this before.

"Come on, honey, just pony up. We're all adults here," Michelle wheezes.

"No, really, it's for my sister."

Crimson glances at Michelle and they both laugh.

"No, what I mean is, she's getting married," he says. "Fuck, this is awkward. I swear I'm normal."

Crimson walks over to the young man. "Toy, movie, or clothing?" she asks.

"Oh God. Clothing, clothing, I don't want to know anything else. Something nice, though, I guess. I don't know. You're a girl. What would you like?"

"I'd like a fat rubber cock, one with enough girth to get the job done," Michelle yells.

Crimson giggles.

The guy just smiles. "I was talking to her," he says, pointing to Crimson.

"I guess, from my brother, I'd like something simple, nothing racy."

"That sounds great," he says, stumbling again.

Crimson catches him by his forearms. They are solid. She leans in a bit and notices he smells like beer, cigarettes, site, dirt, and Old Spice. It has been a long time since she has touched a man.

"You should get her a dick lighter," Michelle says, a new cigarette dangling from her lips. She picks up a small tube of pink gel beside the lighters. "Or some nipple nibbler." She screws off the cap and sniffs. "Mmm, this actually smells good."

"It tingles," Crimson says. "Most women use it as lip gloss."

Michelle squeezes the tube until a glob catches on her finger. She wipes it across her mouth. "Yummy. How about a kiss, ah...?"

"Danny."

"How about a kiss, Danny? Free of charge." Michelle leans forward, her slinky tank top billowing open to show a pink lacy bra cupping impressive tits.

"No, that's cool. I'm not into tingly stuff," he says, his eyes on Crimson.

Crimson smiles. She notices his eyes are green. Her heart hammers in her chest.

"Fine, I guess I'll just have to entertain myself," Michelle says, turning to the TV.

Danny steps in close to Crimson. "What was your name again?"

Crimson looks up at him through her eyelashes and says her name.

He smiles. The lines around his eyes make him more handsome.

"Well, Crimson," he says, his face hovering above hers, "let's find something you'd like."

She shivers. She doesn't want to be attracted to him, but the way his hair catches on the scruff on his chin makes her legs weak. He licks his lips and her breath comes in a shallow gasp.

"Uh, we, um." She steps back. "We have some nice stuff over here, on this rack." She turns and walks away from him. He follows her, humming along with the radio.

When she gets to the rack, she pulls out a pair of pale yellow panties with white bows.

"You like those?" he asks.

"They're nice," Crimson says, meeting his eyes.

"Okay, I'll get them."

She smiles as he takes the hanger from her. He leans in, pinning her in place, and reaches past her. His face grazes her cheek for a second before he leans back, and she sees him holding the matching bra.

"You gotta get the set, right?" he says.

"Yeah, I guess you do, if you're that kind of brother." She exhales.

"I am."

"Oh, man, look at that guy's dick," Michelle yells, "it's like a toddler's arm."

Crimson slips past Danny and walks to the front of the store, avoiding Michelle's swinging legs to get to the till. Danny follows her again, puts the lingerie down on the counter, and stares at her. She wishes they were alone.

"When are you off?" he asks.

"I, uh, seven a.m."

"Wanna go for breakfast?"

Crimson checks her watch. "That's in four and a half hours. Aren't you tired?"

"I'll go home for a nap."

"Okay. Seven sharp, though, or I'm going home."

"Deal."

She wraps the lingerie in tissue and places it in the store's usual black bag. As she hands over his purchase, he places his hands, warm and rough, over hers.

"See you at seven, Crimson," he says, heading out of the store. The pavement outside the door is bathed in green neon light.

When the door shuts, Crimson turns around to find Michelle leaning forward with a huge smile.

"He is fucking hot, babe."

"He is, right?"

"Yeah, and he looks like the guy in your fucking book here," she says.

"It's weird, right? Getting picked up in a porn store?"

"Nah, I found my last boyfriend at my last strip club. When you meet someone, you just gotta go for it."

"I guess."

"Hey, look, I gotta go. I'll be back tomorrow. You can help me find stuff that'll make a guy cum in his pants." Michelle hops off the counter. She hoists her big purse, then pulls out another cigarette and slides it between her lips. "Maybe your luck is changing. Maybe this guy'll take you far away from this hole and you'll become a famous artist."

"Maybe."

"Everything'll work out. I'm sure of it. See you tomorrow—I'll bring you a poster."

Michelle pushes the door open and walks out. Before it closes all the way, Crimson sees her cupping the cigarette with one hand and flicking the dick lighter with the other.

/

Crimson is filling in the details of her sketch when the door opens.

Danny stands in the entrance. His smile is sloppy as he lurches into the store.

Crimson looks at her watch: it's only 5:19 a.m.

"Hiya, honey," Danny says.

"Hey, it's only twenty after five. I'm not off for a while still," Crimson says.

"I just wanted to surprise you."

"Okay," Crimson says, standing.

Danny walks to the middle of store. "Come here. I gotta show you something."

Crimson frowns. "You been drinking?"

"I went home and had a few beers. I only live a few blocks away. But I was still wired so I thought I'd just come back and say hey."

Crimson doesn't want to leave the emergency button so she stays in place.

Danny's smile widens. He takes a few lumbering steps toward her. At the counter he leans over and grabs her hair to drag her in for a kiss. Their teeth smash together, his tongue presses against hers, and she gags. She pulls away from him, afraid.

"You're so pretty, Crimson. And your name is like fire."

"Thanks."

"I mean it. You're like the prettiest girl in Fort Mac. You could totally be a stripper."

Crimson's heart is racing, but not from desire. The reek of beer wafts over her and makes her stomach churn.

Danny backs up a few paces before swivelling his hips. "I want to show you something." He fumbles with his belt. Crimson presses the emergency button, but finds it is jammed. His pants drop around his ankles. "Do you like them?"

He is wearing the panties. His dick is squished in and his balls are falling out the sides. His pubic hair curls around the lace.

Crimson hits the emergency button again, but it doesn't give. She backs away, bumping the TV.

Danny pulls up his shirt to reveal the matching bra.

"You said you liked these ones, right?" He wiggles around.

"Oh my God."

Danny turns, stumbling and falling to his knees. The panties ride up his ass crack. He laughs, then pulls down a rack of movies to the floor as he stands back up. He grunts from the effort.

"Come on, babe, why don't you come over here? They're soft, you can feel."

Crimson is in shock. Everything is wrong. She lunges for the phone. He lurches to the counter before she can get to it. The shirt hides the bra, but his pants are still pooled around his ankles. He smiles at her, but everything handsome in his face is gone. All she sees is paste-white, clammy skin, unfocused eyes, movements that are too exaggerated.

"Please, you have to go," she whispers.

"What?" he says, leaning his elbows on the counter.

"You have to go," she says louder.

"Why? Don't you like me anymore?" There's an edge to his voice.

"It's just my boss—there are cameras and he'll get mad," she says.

Danny almost falls again. "Oh, okay, I get it, babe. I'll come back at seven, we can have breakfast at your place." He winks.

"Sure," Crimson says.

He bends over and pulls up his pants, which keep falling back down as he tries to walk. He smiles again and waddles to the door before pushing against it.

"See you at seven," he mumbles.

/

Crimson tries to take a deep breath. Her legs feel weak but she forces herself to walk to the front door. She latches the door shut and leans against it, trembling. She can hear Danny out on the road singing.

When his voice fades, she leaves the door. She steps over the movies he scattered. Her vision is blurry. She walks behind the counter, grabs her sketchbook, and rips the picture out, then tears it into pieces. A scream escapes her. She throws the book at the lighter display. Miniature penises fly through air and land on the floor with the movie cases.

Crimson sinks down and holds her arms close to her body. Why does everything lovely transform into a black, churning disaster?

The moaning continues behind her.

It's this town, she thinks. If she leaves, then everything will be okay. She will be okay. She just needs to get away.

Crimson hauls herself up and walks past the lingerie, now dusty and cheap, fit only to be ripped off. She eyes the cash register. She punches in a non-existent sale and stuffs every bill and all the coins into her pockets. She glances up at the camera but decides she doesn't give a fuck.

Crimson picks up her sketchbook. She kicks the penis lighters out of her way as she walks to the door. She steps outside into the dawn air. The sun is just starting to rise. The green neon light from the strip club sign is fading. She heads toward the Greyhound station. Her boss and the cops will never find her. She'll disappear. She'll become someone better.

EVERY DROP FROM THE FAUCET IS GOLD

The future.

It looks like the desert has swallowed the entire Earth. Gasping mouths inhale the hot thick air, longing for a drop of moisture to calm their swelling tongues.

That's what I see in my dreams. These aren't nightmares. These are predictions. I know you think that sounds fake, that I am making something up, but I assure you, it's all true.

When you turn on the tap, I bet you don't even think about all the water you waste. How much water do you really need, to wet your toothbrush? A few drops maybe? How much do you actually waste down the drain? Too much.

How many glasses of water do you pour but never finish? How many times have you let your kids water the driveway, or the sidewalk, or the fucking decorative stones you have lining your lawn? How much water has your child wasted?

At night I wake up in a world without the luxury—yes, what we have is a fucking luxury—of water. I see your kids, the same ones you let water the pavement, I see those kids as bleached bones.

They'll all die, you see?

Your kids will fucking die because they don't have enough water. And you don't fucking care.

No one cares. No one, not even me when I take a bath and then just let the water drain, not even me when I let my mind wander as I overfill a pot and I have to pour some out. Not even me when I make tea I don't drink, or when I wash my hands and let the water swirl around my fingers for a few seconds more than necessary, or when I flush two times because there is a tiny scrap of paper lingering in the toilet bowl.

In my dreams, as I crawl through the barren world we have created, I think back on all the water wasted in my life and I curse every single fucking one of us.

STARTING A RELIGION

You lay the foundation for your burgeoning religion in a manifesto of sorts—even though you've never read one before.

On Space and Time, Faith, and Eternity

Our lifetime is but a day. A blink, if you will, in existence. Days are just an illusion—as is all of time—you go unconscious at the end of the day because your body demands it, but time does not stop. Your life continues from the moment you are conceived to the moment you die. And just as you lose consciousness every night, death is but a loss of consciousness of life—until we are reborn into the next day of our existence. There is no stopping, no halting. From the moment everything was created to the moment everything is uncreated, we are as we are.

You decide it's time to share with someone all the thoughts that have been bouncing around in your head. It's surprising, their reaction. They take you seriously. And then they pass your manifesto on to other people. The next thing you know, you're sitting in a small dark room with a few faces pointed at you—you're talking and they're listening.

> This life is only a grain in the expanse of time—and in your soul's experience. Only with this realization can we truly begin to strive for our higher purpose.

You've often thought about what the world is really made of. You've often felt like you've been here before. That this isn't your first go around on the wheel. That you've been here so many times before that life is just boring now. You wonder why you choose to come back again. You wonder if you had a choice.

But then you wonder if you're just being stupid. Does reincarnation actually exist? Maybe not. But that's the thing, though. No one really knows for sure. And everyone wants to. In that deep place inside, we all want to know everything. Because we know almost nothing.

> But we must ask ourselves, what is our higher or true purpose? Well, there are two types of higher purposes.

You only needed one person to believe, but now you have many. You cannot understand why they think so highly of you. You are nothing. So you wait, lurking in places they won't suspect you, waiting for them to start speaking words against you when they think you absent.

Sitting on the roof of the derelict building you've moved into, you stare at the dark sky and think. Think of new things to say, revising and editing in your mind. There is new pressure on you now. You have to perform. You have to be better, wiser than the rest.

Dirt creeps up higher on your arms every day. You have no time to bathe, only to splash a bit of lavender oil under your armpits. Shadows elongate your face. You can't stop now, you can't leave, they need you. You need them.

> One: this relates to the whole of your exis-
> tence. This purpose is unknown. There are
> many different theories floating around out
> there, but do not listen to them. We do not
> know this purpose and that is okay. If we are
> to know it, what we do in this blink of life
> would be completely useless.

You step into the centre of the circle—at least, that's what you think you do. In reality, you stumble forward, trip-ping on the corner of the green robe you decided to wear because you thought it made you look dashing. You recover only slightly before making it to your mark. Once there, you hoist your hands and declare in a practised voice: *Reality is not what you perceive, nor is it what you believe; reality is nothing, and nothing exists because everything exists.*

You pull your hands down and gaze around the circle. You catch the eyes of each one of the thirty or so nodding heads that surround you, those who have been feasting on your words for the last few months.

You hate them.

The cloying admiration they surround you with both repulses you and keeps you locked in their circle. It keeps you locked inside your room day and night. It locks you in front of your mirror, in the reflection of your own eyes, in your voice as you practise the words that tumble out of you.

You hate them, but you cannot be rid of them.

They believe in what you say.

You don't even fully believe in what you say, but having others do so feels nice. It feels better than before, when you were alone with the writing in your journal. It feels better than banging your head against the wall in an endless existential crisis.

It feels nice to be needed.

> Two: this blink, this grain of experience, this time is for us to learn. There is something, maybe it's just a kernel, maybe it's a whole mountain, but there is something you have to learn to push yourself further along your journey to becoming a whole being. Once you've learned it, you'll blink into another consciousness; you'll be on to the next lesson, the next step in your journey.

You wonder, in your idle moments, if perhaps we're just parts of a machine, and that our time on Earth is just a vacation from our actual life. That every part of the machine gets a vacation and we can choose, from a bright and flashy pamphlet, the era in which we'd like to visit Earth. We live an entire lifetime on our vacation. Pain, sadness, love: it's all part of the package. And when we die, it's really just the end of our vacation. We're back to work. And we dream then—we dream of when we'll live next. Will we be a citizen of Rome? A ruler in the mighty era of Drand? Will we revisit other parts of the machine we've fallen deeply in love with again, and again?

Sometimes you believe this is the truth. Sometimes it scares you to think that you're just a small cog in the vast machine that is the universe.

But if this is true, you have to wonder: Why did you choose to come here? To this place in time? Was it truly to be a leader of the masses? Do you possess all of this knowledge because you're supposed to? Are you supposed to start another true faith? Did you circle that in your vacation application? Did Jesus?

> There are times when someone is forced into the next blink without learning. By being wrapped up in each nanosecond of life, by fighting for something people perceive as remotely important, by focusing energy on things that have literally no meaning, people lose sight—and lose their chance—at the learning.

The first thing you have to understand, you hear yourself say, is that time does not exist. A murmur of agreement echoes through the sweat-slicked bodies of the people sprawled out on the hard, unyielding concrete floor. So, what then is space composed of if not time?

You watch them ponder this ridiculous question you've posed. How can they still not understand what you're doing? How can they still believe, and how can more people be flocking to this deserted concrete dump in the middle of nowhere?

You shake your head before gliding toward the doorway that leads outside. The bright ring of sunlight flickering through the door's outline beckons you to leave this place you've created. But you cannot. You feel their eyes drawing you back in, pleading with you for more. Always more.

> Some people are so far away from their souls that they cannot perceive anything apart from what feels good in the moment. These people will take from others with

no thought. They will be greatly saddened
in the next blink. They are so lost. They
must find their own way. You cannot force
anyone to step back and consider themselves. You can only view the whole of
yourself and your time living.

You feel the pressure rising. They want even more from you.
You sit in the chair in the corner of the room. It's all getting
to be too much. There are rows of bunkbeds now in the
basement, filled with people you don't recognize. They are
repeating your words. You've begun to read words written
by Einstein and other physicists to fill in the gaps in your
imagination. This has only brought you more followers.
Your hands tremble all the time now.

In this blink, everything is an illusion *and*
everything is real. Everything *and* nothing
matters.

You think about how other religions have been created by
ordinary people. Writers, woodcarvers, meditators—you
name it, they've all created something. They've provoked
war and death. Genocide. Peace and goodwill, hope.
Fear, control, love. Anyone can create anything. Why
shouldn't you?

So, to that end, know that everything
humanity has created is nothing. This soci-
ety that we all live in is false. It may fall apart
around us—it may not. That doesn't really
matter. Just knowing it's all false can pull
you out of the nanosecond. It can relieve

you of the pressure put on you—for none of it matters. It doesn't matter what you own, who you hate, what you fight for or against. Once we leave this blink, all of that is gone. It will no longer have any meaning for us. These things we surround ourselves with, they do not matter. These countries we fight for, these forms of civilization, all of it is artificial. Just look backward: how many empires have fallen? How many religions? How many societies and civilizations? They did not survive, and neither will ours.

Do not let this discourage you, and do not run to death as an answer, for it is just another step, another blink. Nothing is solved by just dying. You will still have to learn the lesson you need to learn.

You stand in front of your multitudes. Everything has happened too fast. Your mouth is dry. You ball your hands into fists to hide the shaking. The lights stab your eyes and slice through your brain, erupting in a throbbing ache that never ceases. You close your eyes and focus instead on the ebbing roar of the mass of people surrounding you. They all want so much from you. They need to know more, always more. You have given all that you have. There is nothing more you can impart. You know nothing else. They memorize all your movements. There is someone always following you, writing down everything you spew. You are now just repeating the same thoughts you've always had, over and over again, each time getting further and further away from that truth you once thought you knew.

You just needed one follower—not all these others. But you cannot hide now. They are always there; they are always watching.

They have made you into something you are not, and you love them for it. Even as you hate them for it too.

Step back. Once you understand what I have written, you will find peace.

SPECTRE SEX

The memo was slipped through the crack between the rocks that served as Damien's door. As always, it was done by an unseen hand, just as dusk faded into true night. The crinkle of the paper—the only indication anything had changed in his little universe—meant just one thing: time to go to work.

He pushed his head deeper into the pillow. He just wanted to rest. Years upon years of memos. Nights upon nights not his own. He wished he had the convenience of calling in sick like alives did. He'd never fully appreciated the luxury of being able to fake-cough into a phone and fall back into bed—not until after he died.

He inhaled deeply. He liked to spray his meagre pillow with a diffusion of lavender oil he'd stolen from an alive's nightstand. Technically, he wasn't supposed to take things from his clients' homes, but what else did he have to fill his life with? Once an alive invited him in, well, everything was up for grabs.

When the deepest, blackest, darkest part of night finally fell upon the ground he called home, he knew it was time, and he couldn't put off leaving any longer. He swung his legs over the side of his cot—another thing he'd borrowed from a client's garage. Damien checked the clock, yet another theft. He'd dawdled too long, leaving no time for coffee. He stood at the rocky entrance of his home and pushed his essence through the cracks until he manifested on the other side. He hated the feeling of jelly he always became in the middle. How loose he felt, how slippery, like he might not come back together just right.

He walked through the city, his feet light upon the crumbling sidewalks, not disturbing so much as a single pebble. As much as he loved his bed and the solitude it provided, he enjoyed his nightly meandering through the almost-empty city. The way the flickering flames from the ornate metal street lamps splashed light against the dry, decaying grass; the way the city fell so silent, overlaid with the darkness of night. As an alive, he'd never had the nerve to venture out this late, preferring the safety of his home, of electricity and entertainment. It was only now, when all of that had fallen away, that he fully appreciated the sense of calm darkness brought. And truly, no one much was ever around anymore, most residents having drifted away to the larger, newer—soul-sucking, in his opinion—cities to the east.

Damien slipped into the break room, hoping for once that Barry, the red-faced once-lawyer, would already be gone. No such luck.

"Hey, HEY, look who finally decided to show up?" Barry's laugh was like a punch to the ear drums—loud, hokey, and fake.

"Just getting some coffee." Damien poured some of the thick black tar into a mug.

"Need some pep, eh? I never needed that stuff when I was in your biz, I could go from house to house, woman to woman"—he paused to wiggle his eyebrows—"all natural."

Barry liked to think, because he had moved into General Hauntings, that he was somehow better than all those still in the Pleasure department. But in reality, anybody could do general haunting. They were all the same. All you had to do was move some mugs, open a door, show your face in a mirror—boring.

The only benefit Damien could see to General Hauntings was that you didn't have to listen to hours of moaning every night. Or watch a woman perform ridiculous rituals to get you to come to her bed, when you were already there just waiting for her to calm down and go to sleep already.

At least he didn't have to work the ghostly calling boards anymore. That had been fun at first, scaring kids, but it got old after a few weeks when he realized he didn't have any real power, and all they ever asked was if someone was there.

"So you gonna get lucky tonight? A newbie?" Barry asked.

Damien rolled his eyes. "I haven't checked the board."

A deeper voice chuckled behind him. "Ah, you always get the newbs."

Damien turned around as a swirling cloud of dark greys and blues entered the room. It was Chuck, one of the only ghosts he considered a friend. Chuck was in Dreams, which gave him his ephemeral appearance—he was always partly somewhere else, a state that often made it hard to have a full conversation with him.

"He does, doesn't he?" Barry was laughing so hard his eyes looked like they were going to fall out. "He—he always gets the newbs, right, Chuck? Lucky Duck, Lucky Chuck, Lucky Buck—"

"Take a breath, Barry, geez," Damien said.

"Why? Do you think I'm going to d-d-die!" Like the actual flesh of his body, Barry's laughter quivered.

Damien turned away, disgusted. They were all just pooling snot, ghosts.

"So," Chuck asked him, "you hear from up top about your transfer?"

He wished Chuck had kept his mouth shut.

Barry interrupted. "You applied for a transfer? You can't transfer, you've only been in Pleasure for"—he pulled out the small red notebook he kept in his back pocket, flipped to a page, and scanned to the bottom—"20,875 nights. That's way under the minimum."

"Barry, why do you know that?" Chuck asked.

Barry sniffed the air before shoving his notebook back into his pocket. "None of your business."

Damien sipped his coffee. He rolled his eyes and tried not to gag on the bitter brew.

"What department are you hoping to get?" Chuck asked, his nebulous swirling mass floating closer.

Barry leaned in, fingers twitching to grab his pencil and jot down everything Damien said.

"I dunno, maybe something out of the city."

Damien knew exactly what he wanted. There was a plot of land, miles away from anyone else, that needed haunting. It was a solo gig, a monster gig, like a sasquatch but not quite— not a real monster that already existed. Damien could invent his own creature to become, as long as he scared anyone who ventured into the territory and made sure not to get captured on camera. Not getting captured on camera was a general haunting rule. It was a pain for the Erasure department to have to constantly destroy evidence.

"But really," he continued, "I'll just be happy to get out of Pleasure."

"I feel you. I like Dreams. I feel like God."

Damien thought about what it would be like to feel like God. He decided it would be okay as long as he could be God before those seven days and nights.

Damien slipped through the keyhole and into the front entrance of the large mansion. It was as cliché as he could have imagined: giant staircase, table with fresh flowers, neutral colours, high ceilings. Almost like a department store in its blahness. He'd never been here before, and Barry was right—she was a newb. He could sense it, even if he hadn't read it on the board. She exuded hesitant energy.

The first thing he did was walk around the house's ground level, on the lookout for anything he might take home. He walked to the kitchen and pulled open the fridge door. Inside were pans of food wrapped in Saran Wrap—casseroles, loaves, plates of chicken, cake, pies. With mounting horror, he began to suspect this wasn't food she had cooked. The sheer amount indicated condolence food. He whipped around and scanned the kitchen. Dishes piled high in the sink. Empty wine bottles on the counter. Unopened cards stacked on the dining room table.

Shit. A widow. A new widow. Damien groaned. He hated widows. They cried the most when he pushed into them, they clung to his ethereal form, dug their fingers into him as they came not in joy but from extreme loneliness. He hated it. It made him feel so guilty.

At that moment, more than anything in the universe, he wanted to leave. But he couldn't. He could already feel the pull of her from upstairs. She really needed this, and that compelled him upward. He tromped up the stairs, wanted to be able to make enough noise to maybe scare her into not going ahead, but of course his feet didn't make a sound against the thick carpet. When he got to the master bedroom, he sighed, then oozed himself through the crack underneath her door.

The woman was lying naked on her bed, her face hidden in the flickering shadows made by the candles she'd arranged around the room's perimeter. He wished they wouldn't do that; it always made everything smell bad, like dead flowers. He didn't know where alives got the idea that flames did anything to protect them. What protected them was the fact that he was there for their pleasure, nothing else.

She was whispering all sorts of things, something about honouring the deities or the full moon or some other garbage. He slipped into bed beside her and felt the mattress sigh, not that he weighed much, not really—he was more of a gentle pressure. He laid back and stared at the ceiling, waiting for her to finish whatever incantations she thought she needed. When she finally fell silent, he rolled over onto one elbow and let his eyes roam her body. Her nipples were hard; he blew cool air onto them and saw her tremble. He hadn't had much sex when he was alive, never really felt the need, but in death he had become a great lover. Or so he assumed—he always stayed until the woman came, which he figured was really the main secret to being a great lover.

He slid his hands along the sides of her body, letting his fingertips tickle her flesh. Her mouth gaped in a moan and her legs opened; he let his fingers slip into her sex, feeling her wetness. His eyes wandered the room as he stroked her. He noticed the pictures on her walls were all covered in scarves. He wanted to get up and uncover them, but her hips were bucking the air. He wondered if he might get away with just his hands tonight—maybe he wouldn't actually need to have sex with her.

He saw that the closet doors were open, that half the closet was empty—the hangers, the space on the floor for shoes, even the overhead shelf, all were bare. He moved his hand faster, applying more pressure. Surely she would orgasm soon. He slipped a finger in, rocking her from the inside. Her fists gripped the sheets. Her moans were no longer moans; she was panting into her pillow.

Damien noticed then that vases surrounded her bed, and that all the flowers were dead. He could smell the water moulding. He felt sad for her, so he withdrew his hand and undid the zipper of his pants. He moved until he was over her. She was breathing deep, and just as she started to chant again he pushed into her, and in one thrust, he filled her. She screamed out and wrapped her legs around his insubstantial form. He wanted to make her sadness go away and he'd never felt that before, so he moved in time with her hips, and when he thought it might never end, she finally came in one long shuddering moment.

Damien rolled off her. He couldn't actually orgasm himself—sex wasn't even pleasurable to him, really—so he put his penis back into his pants and re-zipped before standing up. Meanwhile, she'd pulled the sheet over her body and was crying into her hands.

He felt bad. He'd wanted her to feel good, but instead he'd made her feel worse. It's possible she'd thought she was having sex with her dead husband, until he'd moved inside her, and she realized that it wasn't her husband after all.

He walked toward the door, but before he could ooze out he heard her stir behind him. He turned and saw she wasn't old. A young widow. Quite pretty, in a soft way.

"Show yourself," she whispered, before adding, "please."

It was the pure loneliness in the *please* that got him. Fuck. The higher-ups would get mad at him if he did what she asked, but she looked so pathetic, sitting there with the sheets drawn up around her, arms trembling as she hugged her sides. He debated oozing out anyway; it would easier, he'd take a casserole from the fridge on his way out. But he knew he couldn't do that to her.

Damien took a form she could see. He could never be truly solid, but this was the closest he could get, a hazy but still-there human shape.

She gasped and pushed back against the headboard.

He grinned and glanced around the room, looking for a tissue box to pass to her.

"How... I don't... I didn't think..." She spoke haltingly, her eyes wide.

"I know, right?"

"You're real."

"Kinda." He rested on his knees at the foot of the bed in front of her, realizing this was actually the first time he'd taken form with a client.

"And you're here—" She couldn't make herself say it, he could see that, even though she'd been the one who'd put the call out to the universe.

"To have sex with you, yes."

"And you're...a devil then? I'm going to hell?" Fresh tears budded in her eyes.

"No, just a regular guy. And I don't think you'll go to hell for something like this. You have no idea how many people do this."

"I got the directions off the internet."

He tried not to roll his eyes but he couldn't help it.

"What? It worked, didn't it?"

"Not really."

"But you're here."

"Because you pulled me here with your need."

"I don't understand."

He shrugged, eyes lingering on her hair. It was dark brown, but not dark enough to be considered black. "Why would you even want to? Trust me, if you understood, you'd be miserable."

"Do you do this often?"

He sighed. "Yeah."

"Why?" Her tears had stopped, at least, and she didn't look as afraid.

He wasn't allowed to tell her that when you die, you get put to work. Alives weren't supposed to know—it was too depressing—the truth, that life was the free-floating fun part of existence, and death was where work really began.

So instead he said, "I do this because I like it." The lie was like rotting meat on his tongue.

She looked at him, really looked at him. "You're handsome."

"Maybe."

"Why are you wearing clothing?"

"It makes me feel normal."

"But you're really dead."

"Yeah."

"And you were once alive?"

He didn't want to keep talking about himself. It would only lead to him letting her know too much. He'd always been a terrible liar. "When did your husband die?" he asked. Her tears started again, and he cursed under his breath. "Sorry, you don't have to answer that."

"I thought he'd be the one who'd come."

Her husband was probably working some menial job, maybe a time-cleaner or something. He surely wasn't a pleasure ghost already, but Damien couldn't tell her that, so he just shrugged. "Can I have a casserole?"

"You need to eat?"

"No, I just like to sometimes."

"How is that possible?"

"I dunno."

He'd been wracked with so many of these same questions when he'd first died, but when he realized that no one knew the answers, he stopped asking and decided to accept everything as it was. Like the first time he found a memo in his pocket. It arrived before he even had a door for it to be slipped under; he'd been sleeping in a park then. The memo was for his first job, deliveries. He went to the address on the bottom and that was it. And every night after that he had a new memo, a new task. Every night. For eternity, he assumed. He'd met ghosts thousands of years older than him still getting memos.

"You can take whatever you want," she whispered.

"Never say that to a ghost, we're all thieves and hoarders."

"When will I ever have a chance to talk to another ghost?"

He could see by the gleam in her eye that she'd be calling for pleasure ghosts frequently enough that she might be able to get another to manifest their form for her. Especially with her eyes being so wide and so blue. He wanted to stop talking to her. Now that she was less sad, he didn't feel so bad for her. He just wanted to be alone again.

He started to dissipate his form.

"You're leaving?" she cried out, hands reaching for him.

"Sleep." He laid his wisp of hand on her forehead, and she fell back into her pillows.

He decided to blow out all the candles before he left. He didn't want her to lose her house along with her husband. Afterward, he pulled a cheese-and-tuna casserole out of the fridge. He ate it with his fingers as he walked home.

The light of dawn was just starting to peek out when his head finally hit his pillow, the scents of lemon and lavender washing over him. His eyes felt like lead weights as they closed.

/

The memo appeared under the rock that served as his door by an unseen hand. This was nothing new. Damien sighed into his pillow before reaching across the floor to retrieve it.

To his surprise, it was different from the ones he'd received for the last 20,876 nights. This memo had a new address on the bottom. But it wasn't an address, really. More like a plot of land, miles away from anything else.

I'M A SAD GIRL, BABY

And that's all I'll ever be, a sad, lonely girl on the edge of tomorrow, until tomorrow is really today's death.

You shouldn't fall in love with a sad girl.

You should only ever be falling out of love with a sad girl.

Because I know you want to save me, but no one can. Because sadness is something I was born with; it sticks to me like my shadow. Sadness coats my insides until I'm all slimy and mucky and slippery. Sadness lets you touch me only enough for you to crave more, until I crumble beneath your same fingers that only a moment ago were making me moan.

Because I'm a sad girl, baby.

Never forget that I warned ya.

WHO IS ERIK?

I moved to the city because I believed in fate, in following your gut. But then I saw a penis at the window of my ground-floor apartment, a hand gripped around it furiously pumping, the man's face obscured by the shadow of his hoodie.

I didn't call the police until the next afternoon, and by then it had apparently become my fault, according to the officer who knocked on my door. If I'd called a few hours earlier, maybe the man masturbating at my window would have been the one who was in the wrong, but I hadn't.

So in the morning the cop who came to my house asked me, "What did you really expect, leaving your shades open after dark?"

Rain had wiped away any essence of semen, so they would never find him—the way the police officer looked at me let me know that was my fault too.

I hadn't called the police earlier because I didn't have a phone yet. The man from the phone company showed up to install my land line the following morning. He told me the number I was assigned was an old one. "Been used by lots of folk, I imagine," he said, as I tested the dial tone with an old thrift-store phone I'd bought a few days earlier.

But I didn't tell the officer any of that. I closed my blinds after he left. Took a steak knife from the kitchen drawer and placed it on my nightstand. This seemed easier.

✦

"Hello?" My voice reverberated through the thick plastic of the phone receiver.

"Is Erik there?" A husky voice. A man's voice. A voice that had inhaled smoke every day.

"Who's Erik?"

"You know who he is. I need to talk to him." Phlegm rattled in a chest I imagined to be bony.

"I'm sorry. I don't know an Erik."

"Just tell him to call me back."

/

At night I think I can see an eyeball peeking in between the window drapes and the wall. I lie there, my body frozen. I know then that I would choose flight if I was ever prey. I am prey. In this city of orange lights and broken concrete, needles littered on the ground, flowers rotting in gutters, I am the prey. I wish I knew who was hunting me. I wish I knew what weapons he held in his sweaty hands.

/

"I know you know where Erik is, bitch." A cough before the line clicks dead.

/

I have a feeling now. It's more than creeping dread. It comes from that same place as fate. This feeling crawls up my spine, takes my vertebrae one step at a time like a ladder.

/

"Erik loved me."

Desperation creeped into his voice. I could almost taste it as he exhaled heavily into his receiver. The man's voice was hollow, unconvinced by even his own words.

"But maybe not anymore," I answered.

"Maybe not." A gear shift: "You can't keep him from me."

"Maybe."

/

The phone rang nightly.

"Do you ever feel me watching you?"

"Sometimes," I answered.

/

I began to feel abnormal if my heart wasn't beating fast against my rib cage. I lost weight. I stopped wearing pants.

/

"Erik always knew what you were going to say before you said it. He really knew a person, you know."

"I do."

"I feel like I know you."

"I know."

/

One night I saw a laser beam on my wall. It drew a heart above my bed. I slept with the drapes open by then. The knife in my fist. My body soaked in sweat. I hadn't seen a penis dripping with cum in the window for a while. Just the flash of red over my bed.

/

"Why haven't you been picking up?"
"How did Erik die?" I asked.
"How do you know he's dead?"
"Isn't he?"

/

The first time I sliced into my flesh, it felt like a quivering bowl of lemon-flavoured jelly—the way it split, so easy, so even, the blood bursting out like a fresh lemon spits out juice.
"I like your skin scarred like that. I like it raw. Open to me."
"I know."
"Erik liked that too. He would cut into this gum line sometimes."
"I'll pull my teeth."
"Save me the saliva."

/

The phone stopped ringing all the time. I pulled the phone into bed with me. I held the hardness against my ear, pushed into the soft flesh. Trying to hear something. Anything.
I slipped the knife into my flesh between the surface and bone.

/

The phone rang one more time.

"Hello?"
  "Hi."
  "Is Erik there?"
  "Speaking."

ASMRRRRRRRRRRRRRRR

To relax now, I watch people on YouTube organize their makeup boxes, pencil cases, art supplies. Instead of drawing a bath and drinking wine, I lie in bed with my laptop propped on my chest and stare into the screen. My head tingles and my toes curl while I watch manicured hands sort through used tissue paper. I fall asleep every night to paper gliding over smooth surfaces. I dream of nothing I can remember.

You'd roll your eyes to the back of your skull if you saw me, naked under my covers, one hand stroking my inner thigh as I watch closets become tamed, junk dumped.

Throw your hands up into the air when I slide my fingers into my pubic hair as a pile of Christmas presents gets wrapped in July.

Scoff and fling yourself toward the door as I circle my clit and watch buttons sorted into piles governed by colour, size, and style.

You'd slam my door shut and yell *fuck* in disgust if you saw me plunge my fingers into myself furiously and pump as a woman sorts and cleans her purse.

You would leave forever if I came in a rush, the last remains of clutter finally purged from behind an old couch.

COMPLEX 2675

1A

Mary dreamed she died.

She woke drenched in sweat, her breath slipping in and out. Something was different. She swung her feet over the edge of her bed and crept into the bathroom. She needed to see herself. With trembling fingers, she flicked the light on, but at the last second avoided her reflection with a quick snap of her neck. Because what if nothing was different and she'd imagined everything? But no, she'd dreamed she had died. So Mary leaned into the space between herself and the mirror, her face still cocked to one side, and pushed her body forward until she felt her stomach stretch over the hard counter. She put a hand on the mirror to brace herself, then turned her head.

Her eyes looked back into her. They startled her. They were alive.

Mary's fingers were still trembling at four-thirty as she straightened the painting of the cottage in the hallway outside Gerry's apartment. She'd hung up the painting because it made her think of the cottage she would've loved to retire in if she hadn't already bought an apartment out in the middle of the prairies.

The ding of the elevator made her heart jump. She grabbed the broom she'd leaned next to her and pretended to sweep the hallway.

Swoosh, the door opened, and Gerry from 4A stepped off onto the pink linoleum. His eyes were focused on the floor. Her heart beat faster as he lumbered toward her. Gerry was a tall man; Mary liked that. He was also quiet and kind. Mary liked that too.

As he approached, she opened her mouth to speak.

Gerry's phone went off. He reached for it, fumbling in his pockets as he did.

Mary's face turned red. She held her breath.

"Uh, hello. Oh hi, Rebecca," Gerry said. He paused outside his door with his back to Mary.

Mary faked a sneeze.

Gerry looked over at her, and she smiled and waved.

When you have a second, she mouthed.

He smiled back at her as he uh-huh'd to the person on the phone, then reached into his pocket for his keys.

Mary cleared her throat and stepped forward.

Gerry pulled his key out and inserted it into the lock. He looked back at her, face tight with a smile, before stepping inside.

Mary waved to Gerry as he shut the door in her face.

She stared at his closed door, waiting for him to get off the phone and come back out and excuse his rudeness. After a few moments of silence, she returned to her broom. She started to sweep the hallway, still waiting for Gerry from 4A to reappear, waiting until she could tell him about her dream, about her eyes that were still alive.

4A

Gerry snapped the phone closed. There was no call—he had programmed his alarm to go off like a phone ringing. Every day he got off the elevator and Mary was there wearing a sickly sweet smile and sharing some inane gossip about one of their neighbours. He'd never seen her leave the building; she was forever in the hallway, sweeping the damn floors. He'd thought about moving just to get away from her, but he was half convinced she'd track him down just to tell him Mrs. Chickamore in 4D had brought home another cat.

He had to be polite, though. She had some disease or something. She nattered on about it all the time.

Gerry dropped his coat and briefcase on the floor. He hated his apartment, how his head almost touched the ceiling. He kicked off his dress shoes with a sigh and shuffled to the kitchen. All he wanted was a beer and silence. All day at the office his phone had been ringing, the emails had just kept coming. He swore all he ever did at work was answer questions. He didn't even know what his real job was anymore.

The fridge was empty. Gerry slammed the door and filled a glass with tap water, then shuffled to the couch and plopped down with a grunt. He kept the lights off. He'd been waiting all day to come home and sit in the cool darkness of his living room. No questions, no answers, just silence.

Gerry closed his eyes and thought about the girl he'd seen in the elevator on the way up. She was new to the building maybe—he tried hard not to pay attention to the other people who lived in the complex. But he knew he'd never seen her before, and she wasn't a visitor because she had laundry. She looked nice, and she'd smiled back at him. And she was pretty—well, not super pretty, but pretty enough. Her smile was a bit toothy, but he could live with that. And she hadn't asked Gerry any questions. She'd understood his need for silence. No questions, no answers. He wondered what her name was. She'd smelled good, like flowers—maybe lavender, and something else. Lemon maybe.

3C

Sarah banged on the washing machine.

"Fuck you, you fucking piece of shit washing machine."

She pushed the On button over and over again, hoping for something to happen. She gave the machine a final kick before crumpling to the ground.

"Fuck!"

Sarah knew it was just her shitty luck, the same shitty luck that followed her everywhere she went. She had just moved into the building and she already hated it. She hated every goddamn thing about it: the pink linoleum, the cramped elevator with the creep who wouldn't stop staring at her, and now this fucking washing machine.

All Sarah wanted was something good, a glimmer of hope, somewhere. She sat in the dank basement and stared at the floor for a few minutes until the door to the laundry creaked open. She sighed before lifting her head up. A guy started loading his clothes into the only other washer in the room. She cleared her throat and he jumped.

"Shit!" he said. "Fuck, you scared me."

"Sorry," she said.

"What are you doing on the floor?"

"The fucking machine won't work."

"Oh yeah, that one's always unplugged."

"Why?" Sarah asked.

He shrugged before turning back around. Sarah studied his back. He had a nice build. He looked like a runner. A runner with amazing hair.

Sarah crawled around to the back and saw that the plug was lying in a pile of dust. She picked it up and plugged it back in. Then she got up, fished some more coins from her pants, and pushed them into the slot. The light turned on and she pushed Start.

"Thanks for your help."

"No prob," he said.

She smiled at him, but he didn't look up. He pushed the button on his machine and it whirled to life. He backed away from the washer and headed toward the door.

"Hey, sorry to bother you," she started.

He turned back around.

"It's just, I'm new here." Sarah stuck her hand out into the air between them. "I'm Sarah."

He eyed her hand and gave a tight smile. "Michael."

Sarah gripped his hand. "If you're ever looking for someone to go out with, you know, dancing or whatever, I'm in 3C."

His eyebrows shot up and he took his hand back. "Uh, okay."

Michael turned back to the door. When he looked back for a second, Sarah gave him an earnest smile. He walked through the door and let it slam shut behind him.

Sarah watched him go and wondered if something good was finally happening to her.

2D

Michael walked out of the laundry room. He heard the door bang on his way out and winced. He hadn't meant to do that. When he'd walked into the laundry room, she'd been crumpled on the floor. He'd chosen to ignore her, he didn't have the time or the patience—but when she cleared her throat, he'd felt obliged to turn around. He'd known the washer was unplugged because Larry in 2B always unplugged it.

Michael pushed the button for the elevator. It dinged immediately and the doors slid open with a gentle swoosh.

He stepped on, pressed D, and the doors slid closed again. Michael looked at his reflection in the gold-flecked mirror in front of him. He looked tired—his eyes were darkened with bags and his mouth was turned down in a frown. He looked up instead and watched the numbers light up. When it hit the lobby, the doors opened.

Standing in front of Michael was the most gorgeous man he had ever seen.

The man gave him a smile.

"Oh, um, hello," came a shrill voice from behind the man.

Michael saw Mary from 1A standing behind him. She was clutching her broom and smiling her sickly sweet smile, one hand outstretched like a claw, motioning for the man to come to her. Michael felt his stomach tighten as the man turned toward her. Michael reached down to push the button to keep the door open, but before he could, it slid closed.

1A

Mary rubbed her thumb up and down the worn wood of her broom as she studied the man in front of her. She'd never seen him before.

"I'm Mary, I live here," she said.

"I'm Gabriel."

"Well, that's a nice name. So you're an angel?"

"Oh, no," he answered.

"So you're a devil then?"

"What?"

Mary laughed, the crack of it echoing around the lobby. "Do you like our building here?" she asked.

"Yeah, it's nice."

Mary watched Gabriel as he took in the lobby. It was her mission this summer to clean it up. She'd been waiting since last summer for Tom, the landlord, to do it, but he'd never gotten around to clearing out all the old junk left by previous tenants. Mary had finally decided that she'd had enough waiting. She would do it herself.

"Well, it will be nice, once I clear out all this junk. I might put some plants in too. What do you think? Do you like plants?"

"Oh, yeah, they're nice," he answered.

"But do you think they would make this lobby nicer?"

"Yeah, sure."

"Are you moving in?"

"Oh, no, I'm just visiting a friend."

"Who?" Mary asked.

Gabriel stuffed his hands in his pockets. Mary knew from a show on TV that this meant he was lying.

"Someone I used to know."

"Well, you know, we all know each other—in this building, I mean."

"That's great," Gabriel said.

"So, you like the idea of plants then?" Mary asked again.

"Yeah," Gabriel said.

"That was Michael."

"What?"

"On the elevator, his name is Michael. He lives in 2D with his wife. They're a nice couple."

"That's great," Gabriel said as he looked past her, out the lobby's large glass window.

Mary gestured to the mailbox. "So, which one of these is your friend?"

Gabriel looked back at Mary and then over to the wall lined with little gold boxes. He took a step forward and pointed at a name written in black cursive.

"Oh, she's on C, come on, I'll take you there," Mary said as she grabbed Gabriel by the elbow. She guided him to the elevator and pushed the Up button. They waited in silence as the lighted numbers ticked down. Swoosh, the door opened and they stepped in. Mary leaned over and pushed C.

4A

Gerry stood at his door, his eye mashed against the peephole as he surveyed the hallway. He hadn't heard the swishing of Mary's broom for quite some time, and thought it might finally be safe to go out and grab a six-pack from the shop on the corner. He opened his door a crack and poked his head out into the hall. It was empty. He stepped out and shut it as gently as he could manage, then slipped his key in and turned it until it clicked. He spun around and headed to the elevator. He pushed the button, and as he waited, he kept an eye on Mary's door. It stayed shut.

Ding.

The door slid open, and the girl from before was tucked into the elevator's corner. He felt his face go red as he stepped in. He pushed the L button and stood facing the door. The elevator started to go in the opposite direction, but Gerry didn't care. He watched her face in the mirror as she twisted the ends of her hair. She didn't pester him with hellos and questions, and he felt his admiration grow.

Ding.

The door opened on C. Gerry moved to the side, and as she walked past him, he breathed her in—definitely lemon and lavender.

She stopped short, and over her shoulder Gerry glimpsed a tall man in a black wool coat standing outside what he guessed was her door.

"Gabriel?" she said.

Gerry held his hand out to stop the doors from closing. He was so focused on her that he didn't see the person standing beside the tall man, waving.

"Gerry!" Mary yelled.

Gerry groaned and tried to melt into a far corner of the elevator.

"It was nice meeting you, Gabriel," Mary said as she took off toward the elevator.

Gerry was obliged to hold his hand out again to stop the doors from closing. He looked past Mary and watched the girl walk toward the tall man. The man looked nervous, and Gerry felt his own face burn from embarrassment for being caught by this man watching her so intently.

Mary stepped into the elevator and immediately started to natter at him. "I'm so glad I ran into you," she said, her voice trembling with excitement. "There are so many things I have to tell you. I had a dream last night."

The doors closed and Gerry slumped against the back wall. The elevator was still headed the wrong way. He looked at the floor. Unlike the rest of the building, the floor was brown.

"Are those new tenants?" he asked, interrupting Mary.

"That was Gabriel, he's a friend of Sarah —"

"Sarah." Gerry felt her name in his mouth.

"—from 3C, she just moved in."

"Sarah."

Ding.

The doors opened on floor D, and Gerry saw Michael from 2D standing in the hallway. He looked like he was playing a game on his phone. He looked up and Mary waved before the doors closed again.

Sarah. Blond hair. No questions.

2D

Michael was hyping himself up. He'd been standing out in the hall playing Tetris on his phone, willing himself to open the door and go inside. Only after the elevator had come and gone, opening and closing on Mary's smile, did he shove his phone back in his pocket.

He pushed open the door. The apartment was strewn with clothing, garbage, and other useless knick-knacks. He gritted his teeth.

"Michael?" His wife's voice came from the direction of their bedroom.

"What?" he asked.

"Where were you?"

"Doing laundry."

"I said I'd do it."

"But you didn't."

"What's that supposed to mean?" she asked.

"What do you think?"

"Fuck you," she yelled.

Michael exhaled and walked into the living room. He kicked her crap out of the way and headed for the couch. He flopped down and leaned over for the remote to click the TV on.

"DO YOU OR SOMEONE YOU KNOW NEED LIFE INSURANCE?"

He turned the volume down.

Michael hated everything about his wife. He hated her face, her voice, her disgusting mess. The cloying citrus candles she was constantly burning to cover the smell of cat litter and garbage. The way she kept the volume on the TV blaring. He just fucking hated her.

He sat on the sofa, clicking through the channels, wondered who the tall guy in the dark wool coat in the lobby was.

3D

Martha, just breathe, she told herself. One, breath, two, breath, three, breath, four, breath.

Martha closed her eyes and concentrated on the feelings in her lungs. I will not panic. I will not panic.

"FUCK YOU."

Martha's eyes popped open as the fight carried over from her neighbours' apartment. She hated them and they loathed each other. She was sure that Michael was into guys and that Vanessa, his wife, was having an affair. She'd complained to Tom, the landlord, about their constant fighting, but he said it wasn't his problem—he had to take care of his kids and fix all the other problems in the building, he explained to her in a degrading voice every time she asked.

Just breathe, Martha. One, two, three, four, in and out.

She'd been dreaming about Mark. She thought she was over him, but maybe not. He'd left six months ago, and now Martha had panic attacks. Panic attacks that kept her trapped in her small apartment where the linoleum was an awful shade of puke pink and the neighbours never stopped screaming.

Just get up, Martha. Just get up.

Martha put one foot down on the floor and took a breath. She put the other foot on the floor and felt her muscles tighten.

Breathe.

She stood up and took small steps until she made it to her patio door. She peeked out and saw the sky was grey. That was reassuring; grey meant nothing extraordinary would happen, it meant the same day as yesterday and the same as tomorrow. She felt her pulse steady, and then she heard a noise in the hall. She darted over to the door to peer out the spy hole. A load of books, magazines, and clothes flew out into the hall. She pulled her head back before looking again.

"You fucking asshole."

"Cunt. That's my shit."

"Well, you said you wanted the place clean, right?"

Martha decided to open her door, her curiosity in that moment stronger than her desire to keep hiding. Her hand shook as she twisted the knob; she poked her head out.

Michael was in the hallway, picking up his stuff. She noticed how tired he looked.

"Sorry, Martha," he said.

"Are you okay, Michael?" she asked.

"We're fine," he answered.

"Are you sure?"

Michael glared at her. "Yes."

Martha inhaled sharply and shut the door. She turned the lock and took a step back, and another and another, until she was back in her bed, under her covers. She slowed her breathing and listened as her neighbours continued fighting.

A little while later, she heard new voices. This time they came from outside, on the balcony below hers. Martha wrapped her comforter around her shoulders and stood up. She shuffled to the patio door and slid it open.

"What are you doing here, Gabriel?" asked a woman's tired voice.

"I already told you," a man answered.

"That's not a reason," she said.

"Sarah, please," he said.

Martha stepped into the early evening and felt the spring air blow her hair around. She sat down and leaned against the glass of the door, breathed in the smell of prairies and the rather pleasant smell of the lemon candles Michael's wife was always burning. She didn't know anything about her new downstairs neighbour yet, but she figured they might be better to listen to than Michael and Vanessa fighting.

3C

Sarah heard the suction of the patio door above her open. She didn't know the freak who lived above her, but she'd heard her playing the same song on repeat night after night. Sarah could just picture her looming above them, her ears straining to hear everything.

"I can't go back," she said.

"Why not? I love you," Gabriel said.

"Stop saying that," Sarah hissed.

She looked out at the prairies beyond her balcony. Tall stalks of grass swayed in the evening breeze. The sky was tinged red and orange with the fading sun. She took a deep inhale of the cigarette clutched between her fingers. Gabriel gave her a condescending look, but it only made her smoke faster and deeper.

"I brought your ring." Gabriel reached into his shirt pocket. He held the ring out to her. When she looked away, he grabbed her and shoved the ring into her palm.

She clutched it but didn't turn to look at him. She could feel the heat of his body, his rough fingertips on her wrist. It would be so easy to turn to him, to lean up and kiss his tender lips. To leave her shitty apartment and go back to their home where she had no responsibilities, where she didn't have to worry about paying the rent or buying furniture. But she couldn't do that. She needed something more than what Gabriel could give her—she needed freedom. The ring in her fist felt heavy, and she wrenched her hand back from his.

Sarah threw the cigarette over the balcony and watched it soar over the brown stubble of grass surrounding the perimeter of the building.

"That's really dangerous, you know," Gabriel said.

"I have to go check my laundry."

"Fine." He moved to let her pass.

Sarah stepped inside her bare apartment. There was no furniture yet. She hadn't brought anything that reminded her of Gabriel.

"Why can't you believe that I still love you?" he asked as he followed her inside.

"I don't know, Gabe, I just—I just feel like I need to be away from you, okay?"

"But why?"

"Because I just need to."

Her new apartment was now being tainted by Gabriel's presence. She had to get him out.

"Come on," she said.

"Where?"

"Laundry, remember?" she answered.

"You should leave the patio door open, it's like a furnace in here," Gabriel said.

Sarah glared at him. She walked to the counter and set the ring down on it.

"I brought you some of your clothes from home," he added. "They're in the car."

She sighed. "Keep them." She swung the apartment's door open and stepped into the hallway. Gabriel followed her out.

"Aren't you going to lock the door?" he asked.

"There's nothing to steal," she answered.

They stood in front of the elevator. Sarah kept her eyes on the pink linoleum. She could feel Gabriel staring at her.

Ding.

The doors slid open; they stepped inside. Sarah slouched into one corner, away from Gabriel, as the door slid closed again. She eyed their reflections in the gold-flecked mirrored doors. Gabriel was too handsome for her. That had always been a problem.

When the doors opened at the lobby, Sarah saw that Mary from 1A had cornered someone by the elevator's doors. It was the creepy guy who'd stared at her in the elevator. He looked like he was small-stepping it toward the front entrance, trying to escape.

Then the doors slid closed, and Sarah was again faced with the lopsided image of her and Gabriel.

1A

"Hey, look—sorry, Mary, but I was actually on my way out."

"Oh, where are you going?" Mary asked, moving closer to Gerry.

"You know, just out."

"Did I tell you about my other plans for the lobby?" she asked.

"Uh, yeah, you did."

"What's your favourite type of plant?"

"I, uh, don't know."

"Do you like ferns?"

"Yeah, I guess."

"Me too. But I really have to tell you my dream before you leave."

"I really have to go, but, ah, tell me later, okay?" He pushed open the front door and stepped out into the darkening night. "I'll see you around."

Mary watched Gerry rush down the steps to the parking lot. She watched until he was out of sight, then turned away. Her hands felt empty. She looked around for her broom. She must have left it on C. She walked to the elevator and pressed the Up button.

3C

Sarah slammed the dryer door shut. She was tired of having to explain herself to Gabriel. She just wanted silence. No more questions.

"Why won't you come home?" he asked.

"Because it's your home, not mine. Mine is here."

Gabriel was hurt, she could tell. But he was also playing with his hair too much, which meant something was wrong.

"What?" she exploded.

"I just—I fucking love you so much and I don't know why you're here calling this shitty building your home."

Sarah walked out of the room without waiting for him, her laundry bag slung over her shoulder. She stood in front of the elevator doors, willing them to open, as his slow steps echoed on the concrete behind her.

"Do you at least want the clothes I brought?" he asked.

"No," she said.

"Why not?"

"Because I don't."

"Because you don't love me anymore."

"Jesus Christ."

Ding.

Sarah got on the elevator and Gabriel followed again. She avoided looking at the mirrored doors this time, focused instead on a pebble that was rolling around on the floor and the lingering scent of lavender that seemed to float around the entire building. They stood in silence until the doors opened at the lobby. Sarah stepped off; she didn't want him back in her apartment. Gabriel reluctantly followed. She hugged her arms to her chest as they stood facing one another. She felt tears in her eyes and wished he would just go away.

3D

Martha's stomach was rumbling, so she went to the kitchen in search of some dinner. The sun had set and her apartment was dark. She left the lights off, and as she opened the fridge, its stark brightness lit her apartment. She grabbed a Diet Coke, popped the top, and started to chug. Her mouth, lungs, and stomach burned, but she kept on drinking.

Swish, swish, swish.

Martha knew that sound. It was Mary. She was sweeping the hallway again. Pop in hand, Martha wandered to the door, her comforter trailing behind her. She peered out the peephole and watched Mary. Back and forth, back and forth, back and forth.

Swish, swish, swish.

Martha felt sorry for Mary. The woman was so lonely.

The door to her left opened.

"Oh, hi, Michael." Mary's voice was high with excitement.

"Mary," Michael said.

Martha laughed to herself. She knew how much Michael hated Mary. He ranted about her to anybody who would listen.

"You going down?" Mary asked. She gestured toward the elevator.

"Yep," Michael said.

"Me too, let's ride together."

Michael rolled his eyes and walked toward the elevator. Mary followed and stood beside him, picking at the peeling paint on her broom's handle.

"You know what? I'm just going to take the stairs," Michael said.

"I'll go with you. I could use the exercise."

Martha watched as Michael clenched his jaw and they both moved toward the stairs. He opened the door and Mary walked through.

"I saw Vanessa this morning, she was talking to Larry from 2B, they looked like they were trading secrets—"

The door to the stairs closed, and Martha was left with the empty hallway. She turned and headed to her couch. She sat down, and as she placed her can of cola on the table, she noticed her cellphone lying among the discarded food wrappers.

She bit her lip, then reached for it.

Her heart hammered in her chest as she turned it on and swiped until she found Mark's number. Her breath came in shallows gasps as she decided whether or not she should call him.

RING, RING, RING.

The phone clicked and she heard someone take a breath.

"Hello?" he said.

"Mark?" Martha strained to hear anything. "Mark, it's me, Martha."

Silence.

"Mark?"

Martha breathed.

"Stop calling him, bitch," a woman's voice said. "You're pathetic."

Martha turned the phone off. Her forehead was sweating and she knew it must be red. Her heart hurt in her chest. She looked at the phone, screamed, and threw it at the wall. It cracked and fell to the carpet.

She started to cry.

One, two, three, four. Breathing on counts of four just like her therapist had taught her. Control your anxiety with your breath. One, two, three, four.

2D

When the stairwell door slammed shut, the noise echoed, but it still couldn't drown out Mary's voice.

"—but then I thought, what kind of secret would Vanessa and Larry have?"

"Uh-huh."

"So, Michael, I've been thinking of putting some plants in the lobby—what do you think?" Mary asked.

"I think it's a hazard," Michael said.

"What?"

"I think that too many people could be allergic."

"Well, that's just ridiculous."

Michael shrugged.

"Do you really think so?"

"Yes. I also don't care."

"Well, I think I'll do it."

"Great," Michael said. He opened the door to the lobby.

"Oh, I almost forgot, I have something to tell you. A dream I had last night," Mary said.

"I don't listen to other people's dreams. They're weird and boring."

Mary trailed after Michael, so that he felt her bump into his back when he stopped short. The tall man from earlier was standing by the window talking to the woman from the laundry room; he couldn't remember her name. The man looked like he was on the verge of tears. It was an intimate moment, and Michael suddenly felt embarrassed.

Beside him, Mary clutched her broom. He knew she must be in heaven. He was disgusted and felt the need to separate himself from her. Michael wavered, then walked to the mailboxes. He fumbled with his keys, cursing the noise, and pretended to sort through his envelopes as the couple whispered behind him. His ears burned with shame.

Suddenly, the front doors clanked open, and they all turned to see who it was.

Gerry from 4A walked in with a six-pack of beer in one hand and a piece of jerky in the other. He stopped mid-entrance when he realized they were all staring at him.

3D

Martha opened her eyes to the darkness.

In the silence, she could think. She thought about the way the woman on the phone had snapped at her. She thought about it and she got angry.

Martha stood and let the blanket fall off her shoulders. She walked to the kitchen and flicked on the light, grabbed a black garbage bag, and started to tear through her apartment. She threw anything that reminded her of Mark into it. Frantic, she stumbled against her bed, then noticed the boom box on the nightstand. She reached over to open the tape player and hesitated—Mark's voice—then exhaled and threw the tape into the bag. She marched to her front door and slipped her feet into her slippers. She had to throw out the bag before she lost her nerve. She walked to the elevator and pushed the Down button, fidgeting while she waited. The elevator dinged and the doors slid open. Martha pressed the button for the lobby, avoiding her own reflection and staring at the bag's reflection instead.

1A

Mary clutched her broom in tight fingers. The tension in the lobby caused her to become rigid.

Ding.

The elevator doors opened, and Martha stumbled out with a garbage bag in one hand, the other shoved in the pocket of her sweatpants. She stopped when she noticed the others.

It was a standoff.

Mary knew she had to say something, she had to do something, so she cleared her throat. Everyone swivelled to look at her.

"I, uh, ahem, I had a dream last night," she started.

"Oh, for fuck sakes, enough," Michael yelled. "Enough with your dreams, your gossip, your plants, your garbage nonsense, enough!"

"Don't talk to her like that," Martha said.

"Excuse me?"

"I said, don't talk to her like that." Martha shrank back into the elevator's still-open doorway. The door tried to close, but it slammed against her body before opening again.

"Don't you fucking tell me what to do."

"Hey now," Gerry said.

"What? You know more than any of us how annoying Mary is," Michael said.

"Ah, come on, man, just let it go," Gerry said.

"Now, Michael—" Mary started to say.

"Mary, maybe you should go," Sarah said.

Michael was staring at Gabriel, Gerry was clutching his beer and jerky and staring at Sarah, and Martha stood in the elevator doorway, staring at the garbage bag.

"I had a dream I died last night and I was all alone," Mary blurted. "It was dark and it was so cold. It was so, so cold. I couldn't feel anything. I was so scared. I woke up in a sweat and I couldn't fall back asleep. It was real, you know? It was real. I think I'm different now, I am, I'm different and I'm alive. And you're all alive too. Don't you see? I had a dream that I died." She looked from face to face. "And now I'm alive."

No one moved.

Mary held her breath. Maybe they'd heard her. Really heard her. She looked from face to face. Everyone was avoiding looking at her.

Mary cleared her throat again, to offer more words.

"I think—" Martha said.

"No one—I mean no one—cares what you fucking think," Michael said.

Martha took a deep breath and stepped back into the elevator. The doors slid shut on her and her garbage bag.

Mary shrank back until her knees hit the chair positioned in the corner of the lobby. Steadying herself, the broom against her chest, she sank into the felted cushion.

They hadn't heard anything she'd said. They weren't different. They wouldn't change.

4A

Sarah cleared her throat. Gabriel reached out to her but she flinched away.

Gerry walked past them, his eyes on the elevator. He pushed the button. He glanced back and saw Sarah wipe a tear from her eye before coming to wait next to him, her laundry bag slung over her shoulder.

When the elevator doors opened, he waved her in. She hesitated for a moment before stepping in first. He realized the open package of jerky was making the elevator smell. He wanted to drop it and put a hand on Sarah's shoulder as she continued to brush her tears away, but he didn't want to get jerky grease on her beautiful hair. Gerry hated himself.

Sarah dropped her laundry bag on the floor and opened the top, rooting around until she found a tea towel. She pulled it out, and as she did, a pink scarf drifted to the floor. Sarah didn't notice it and Gerry didn't say anything. She wiped her face with the towel. When the elevator got to her floor, she hauled the laundry bag back up onto her shoulder and exited. She didn't turn around before the doors closed, but that was okay—because before she'd left the elevator, she'd smiled at him in the gold mirror doors.

Gerry stooped over and picked up the scarf. He held it to his face and inhaled. Sarah. He stood up, smiled, and pushed the letter A. And as he watched the lights flash, he twisted the scarf between his fingers.

2D

Michael turned toward Gabriel, who was wiping away tears of his own. Michael wanted to say something to lighten the mood, to make Gabriel feel better, but everything he thought of seemed dumb or trivial, and eventually Gabriel just turned and left the building.

Michael looked over at Mary. She was still sitting on the chair in the corner, but at least she wasn't talking—her eyes were focused on the stacks of clutter in the opposite corner of the lobby.

He walked to the large window facing the parking lot and watched Gabriel shuffle through the gloom, the lamps from the small parking lot giving enough light to see by. When he got to his car he opened a rear door and stared into the back seat. Michael watched him reach in and pull out a garbage bag, which he hurled over his shoulder into the empty spot next to his car. The bag spilled clothing all over the pavement. Gabriel closed the back door, climbed into the driver's seat, then started up the engine and roared out of the parking lot.

Michael focused on his own reflection in the glass. His eyes were doubled, his face longer and older. When he faked a smile, the reflection looked monstrous. He sighed again. Mary was still in the chair. He walked to the elevator and pushed the Down button.

3D

Martha pressed Play on the boom box, and the song Mark had recorded for her filled the apartment. She curled up on the bathroom floor, tightening her comforter around her. Closed her eyes.

Just breathe, Martha thought, just breathe.

3C

Sarah stood in the middle of her empty apartment—except it wasn't empty anymore. It was filled with Gabriel.

She walked to the kitchen counter and picked up the ring. She held it between two fingers for a moment before moving toward the patio. She stepped into the night, felt the cool breeze in her hair. The ring flat in her palm, she thought about what Mary had said about her dream. She lifted her arm to throw the ring into the darkness, but couldn't. Instead, she walked back into her apartment, slipping the ring into her jeans pocket.

2D

Michael leaned against the dryer in the damp laundry room. His fingers were playing Tetris, but his mind was telling his wife he wanted a divorce. His mind was on a certain pair of shoulders in a dark wool coat.

4A

Gerry sat down on the sofa in his dark apartment. He held Sarah's scarf to his nose and inhaled. Tomorrow he would go up to her apartment and he would return her scarf. He would look into her eyes and he would talk to her. He would ask her questions. He would get to know her. Tomorrow.

1A

Mary, alone, hobbled to the elevator. She held her broom in her left hand and pushed the Up arrow with the right. The elevator doors opened and she stepped into the car. She turned to consider her reflection in the glass.

Her eyes—they stared back at her. Looked into her.

She closed them and saw the image of a fern, green and uncurling, alive.

I LOVE YOU

I lied.

Well, it could be more like you lied to me first, and then I just continued the lie.

You said I love you,

so I said I love you,

and then you said, I love you more,

and I said okay.

I can only handle so many lies in a day.

LOVE, TRANSPARENT

I.   You thought the fly was still alive because it kept
        pulsating—no, squirming—over the white of the
        laminate floor. But when it got closer, you realized
        it was only moving because of the maggots push-
        ing their way through its corpse. White bodies were
        squeezing through the cracks in the flesh like dozens
        of blackheads popping at once. You yearned to lean
        closer, to put your ear against the tiny stomach cavity,
        hear the crunch as they broke through. But you kept
        still, watched from where you'd lain down on the
        floor, as they inched their way toward you. Your body
        too heavy to move and meet their wiggling bodies in
        their forward crawl.

II.   In high school I would spy on him as he sprinted
        furtively across the cement behind the school. He
        would wait to emerge from the rusty back door
        until everyone had gotten bored of waiting for him,
        and then he would pump his legs and streak, like a
        multicoloured universe, across the thick pad that
        penned us in all day. I hid and watched because of his
        translucent skin. You could see through it like it was a
        Vietnamese shrimp roll. The lettuce and carrots of his
        inner workings were constantly in motion—quiver-
        ing, expanding, living. He was like a little rabbit out
        of its den, trembling with fear, and for good reason.
        There were always kids waiting for him somewhere.
        They would beat him, turning his skin from clear to

deep red as vessels broke. Blood blooming like flowering tea. Bruises would spread over his translucent forehead like ink spilled on satin. It would feather at the edges.

III.   You felt the heart from the inside. You had to you cut lower than you expected you'd need to. You cut under the rib cage, through the elastic skin there. You pushed and pushed and pushed. You broke the diaphragm, you kept going. You let the miniature flashlight strapped to your wrist guide you through the web of veins and arteries. You moved between the lungs, which had stopped inflating and deflating. It was slippery, because our insides are slippery, and it was warmer than you expected. But you found the heart eventually. It's firmer than you thought it'd be. You ran your fingers over it, squeezed it. The pooling thickness of the blood stayed under your nails.

IV.   The first time I let him put his translucent fingers inside me, tears dripped down my cheeks. He flicked his tongue over the saltiness. I could see the muscles of his jaw flex, watched as his tongue flicked in and out of his mouth past the barricade of white teeth. I could feel the hard ends of his fingertips as they moved in me, and I was crying because he would never be able to see himself like I saw him. When he undressed that first time and pulled away the layers that obscured his skin, I could feel his fear through the barely-there hair on his skin. His trembling was like a seismic reading, illuminating the vibrations deep within his chest cavity. I could see the glow from the lamp behind him. I wanted him to make me bleed for the first time. I wanted to see him streaked with my blood, for it to blend into the bruised flowers on his skin. After, while he was asleep on the floor, I took out my camera and photographed the evidence of our sex. The way our veins had started to grow together, tangled beneath our skin.

V. You slipped your tongue inside his dead mouth. If you had waited too long after death, all you'd have felt was hardness, but the skin was still warm. The body had not yet leaked brown fluid. You wanted to kiss him one last time before his body hit that magic moment when the skin starts to slip. You stuck your tongue in far enough to see yourself doing it.

VI. I began to associate the stares of people on the streets with our love. There was a secret way we moved through the world. It was just me and his skin. I began to name specific veins, grew familiar with their particular pulsing, tracked their pathways through him. There were no more ink stains to get lost in now, though; his tormentors had moved on to new prey.

VII. You realize it's easier to love someone after they're dead. You don't have to deal with anything but the purity of your love. Entwined in your memories and in the space beside his body, you can sleep soundly. With every memory you relive in your mind, with every slide of your finger down his cold cheek, your love only gets stronger.

VIII. And then he hit me with the words that would tear me from him: he said he needed to be away from me. His skin bloomed red over branch-like lines as he forced out the words through those same trembling lips I had pushed against my own so many times before. When he grabbed my mug of hot lemon tea and smashed it against our kitchen tile. I felt pain then, in the same secret place inside of me where fire had raced at his touch. I stretched out my hands, felt my nails dig in as blood pooled into the crescents. He pulled back, but I held on. You can't separate things that have been melded together without destroying them both. It's impossible. He knew this. You could see he knew it in the way his adrenaline pushed blood through his throbbing veins. I wasn't going to let that separation happen. I picked up a shard of the broken mug and sunk it into the translucent skin I loved.

IX. The cloudy whiteness of his eyes reflects your image. Your hands roam his body as he rests stiff beside you. They wouldn't stop, your hands, now that they can travel wherever they want. You press your lips against his cold ones. You won't have to live apart ever again. This was the truest of love you'd ever felt.

X. You left the window open an inch. You need a scrap of life outside the walls of your room. But only a scrap, a sliver, really: a tree's discarded spores, stray laughter from the street, wind carrying the cold. His translucent skin becomes marred by a buzzing black dot. Your hand flings out in a burst of frenzied energy, pinning the fly to the floor, its tiny body a vibration up your arm.

GLITTER LIKE HERPES

"Opinions are like assholes. Everyone's got one and they all stink."

Michelle plunked herself down on the tottering stool in front of the small mirror. Gold glitter shook off like dead skin whenever she moved.

"The trick is to only listen to the ones that matter, the people who matter, who have something really important to say. You feel me?"

The waif-like girl sitting beside her wavered on her stool. Michelle watched the girl burp, betting her throat burned with whisky and bile. She could tell by the crusted mascara flaking off the girl's eyes and the line of faded pink lipstick circling her parched mouth that she'd been up partying all night.

"Honey, here." Michelle handed the girl a makeup wipe and motioned to her mouth. "You've got to decide what you want from life and you have to be okay with it."

The girl pressed the wipe to her mouth before resting her head against the nearby wall. She closed her eyes.

"Stripping is always a good fallback, I'd say that to anyone, even those pinched-faced rich women. You always need a fallback, you feel me? Always. Have an exit strategy no matter what."

Michelle looked the small girl over. She always gave the same-ish speech to the new girls. They never listened, but if she didn't try, she just wouldn't feel very good about herself.

"Honey, you listening?"

"I am," the girl croaked out. "You always need to fall back. Exit."

"You can't depend on a man, that's what I'm saying. They will always, I mean always, leave you. Trust me, honey, you don't want to be caught in a situation where you're married, and he's the only one making any money, and you need him so you can't leave. Never need a man, you feel me? Never need anybody."

"But you need a job, right," the girl slurred. "We all do. And you need a place to live. And you need friends."

Michelle stopped fixing her hair. She looked straight into the mirror, right into the young girl's eyes, which were drooping. "I can tell you one thing with complete honesty: I don't need any fucking job, or any fucking person, or any fucking life. I am the only thing I need." Michelle pulled out a lighter from her purse. It was shaped like a dick and the flame peeked out from the tip. She lit a cigarette and sucked the smoke deep into her lungs. "Also, you're on the schedule for this morning, honey. Pull yourself together."

Michelle hauled herself up off the stool. She adjusted her white tank top, pulling it down to show off the top of her electric pink bra. Her tanned skin glowed with gold glitter. She smiled. She still had it. And that wasn't just her opinion—her purse was filled with cash, cash she'd earned in the only honest way she knew how. She grabbed a bottle off the counter and spritzed her signature combo of bright lemon, lavender, and peppermint oil into her hair, then bent down and tipped the girl's chin up. "Honey," she said, and the girl's left eye cracked open. "Showtime's in ten."

When she let go, the girl's head flopped back down. She let out a small fart, followed by a soft snore.

Michelle began to move fast. Jimmy would be back in a few to collect the girl for the stage. Michelle rifled through the girl's costume bag. She yanked out a pair of panties— black with yellow bows, the ones the girl had been wearing the night before—and slipped them into a large Ziploc bag pulled from her own purse.

Michelle went from cubicle to cubicle, collecting panties—lacy ones, bright ones, small ones, large ones, ones that had small holes. She tucked all of these into the Ziploc bag, except for one pair, a shiny black pleather thong. That one she carefully placed inside the sleeping girl's cubicle, tucked in the very back where she wouldn't notice it. Michelle added a tube of her own lipstick too, just for good measure.

She checked herself out in the mirror again for a brief second, ran her fingers through her hair one last time, then walked out of the dressing room. The swinging door slammed behind her, cutting off the trail of mingling perfumes and fluorescent light. She followed the dark hallway to the club's entrance and pushed the door open. The interior was mostly dark, and pulsing pink, blue, green, and yellow lights hit her in the face. The air clung to her skin. Moist and heavy, it dragged the ever-curling smoke to the floor. The music was pumping, but softly—it was too early for the regulars, just late enough for the been-there-all-nighters.

Tina, an old hand, was twirling lazily around a pole, her eyes focused on the news scrolling across the TV screen behind the bar. Michelle gave her a nod before heading to the bar. She plunked herself down on a stool.

"Whisky," she said, pulling out a cigarette and her lighter.

"Why you gotta always use that damn thing?" asked the bartender, Vinny.

"What? This?" She gestured with her dick lighter. "I like it. You intimidated?"

Vinny rolled his eyes before pouring her drink. "So what do you think of the new girl? What's her name again?"

"Sapphire, I think, or maybe Ruby. I dunno, some damn jewel."

"She doesn't look like a damn Sapphire. More like a cubic zirconia."

Michelle shrugged. "You see her dance?"

Vinny wiped the bar. "Nothing to write home about."

"She'll learn."

"Maybe. I heard Sara talkin', they think she's a thief."

Michelle's heart started to beat faster. She kept her eyes locked on Vinny's and resisted glancing at her bag. "Oh yeah?"

"Yeah. You notice anything missing?"

"No, but I'll check later."

"It's probably just Sara starting drama, she loves that shit."

"Thanks for the drink." Michelle slapped a few bucks on the counter. She never paid for her drinks at the club but she felt like a shit if she didn't at least tip. "I'll see you tomorrow."

"Night off?"

"I think so, yeah. I'm starting to feel a bit sick."

Michelle exited the club. Outside, she felt better. She shook off her discomfort. It would all be okay.

❧

Used panties worn by strippers went for upwards of three hundred dollars each on the dark web. Michelle uploaded a picture of Sapphire's black pair with little yellow bows to her website. She kept the monitor on as she lay back on her bed, meaning to close her eyes only for a second, but nodding off instead. She slept all day, and when she got up that night she discovered someone had already bought the panties. She spent the rest of the night uploading and posting. The sum in her bank account slowly growing.

❧

Michelle stepped off the stage, her legs quivering. Fuck, she was tired. Her blanket was filled with loonies that she hauled over her shoulder like Robin Hood, except instead of giving her money to the poor, she had to give a cut to Jimmy. Michelle always fumed during the walk back to the dressing rooms. Just like a man to hold all the damn cards and take all her goddamn money. But by the time she entered the dressing room she'd be smiling, because she knew, even if no one else did, that she wasn't going to be working at Jimmy's fucking strip club for the rest of her goddamn life. She already had her exit strategy.

The dressing room wasn't too depressing if you didn't look at anything for too long. If you flitted your eyes around the space and only focused on the sparkly costumes, the bright light of the bulbs over the mirrors, the bare flesh of women massaging lotion into their limbs, you'd be mesmerized. At least, that's how she'd felt when she'd first seen the place. Michelle dreamed of opening her own club. She wanted to be a boss. She wanted control, and she wanted her club to be actually pretty, not just move-your-eyes-fast pretty. She wanted to hire only the best girls, the ones without track marks or puffy eyes. She wanted to serve fancy drinks. Play good music.

The dressing room was empty, Michelle being the only girl who Jimmy couldn't afford to force onto the floor. She changed quickly and, before the other girls got back, slipped a few of their panties into her purse. She also tucked a hairbrush with fake diamonds on it in Sapphire's cubicle, again in a semi-hidden spot. Leaving through the club's back door, Michelle lit a cigarette before walking to her car. She had some selling to do.

✒

A rectangle of daylight broke the darkness as two girls tumbled into the club, one holding the other, smaller one up by her elbows. The two men sitting beside the stage blinked in confusion, their warm bubble bursting for the barest of seconds. The young brunette on the stage stumbled against the pole.

"Fuck," one of the girls slurred as the front door slammed behind her. The DJ lazily pushed Play and a new the track came thumping over the speakers. The girl dragged her friend to the nearest booth and pushed her in, giggling. She slid in behind and they snuggled together.

In the murky darkness, Michelle recognized Sapphire and Roxy. She wandered over and plopped herself down in the booth opposite the girls. Roxy had already passed out. Sapphire's fake eyelashes were peeling at the corners, giving her the effect of having large owl eyes. Lines of dirty snow waved up the sides of her dingy white knee-high boots like sedimentary rock, showing the places she'd been. Sapphire waved over to Vinny, her nails glinting green sparkles in the flashing lights.

"What are you doing?" Michelle said, looking at her watch. "It's eleven-thirty in the morning."

"Yeah?"

Michelle pulled out a cigarette. "Yeah, you're supposed to be onstage already."

"I don't want to dance the morning shift anymore. I'm too pretty for that."

Vinny shuffled over and set a glass of water and a mug of coffee down on the table. "Jimmy's gonna be pretty pissed you're so late."

For a second, Sapphire looked like the scared kid she was, but then her face hardened. "I'm not afraid of Jimmy." She said it like someone who'd never been hit before.

Vinny muttered under his breath as he walked away. "You should be."

Michelle looked Sapphire over. She could see the bravado melting as Sapphire started to realize that she might actually be in trouble. "Jimmy don't care about your tits and ass, honey. He's got so many other sets that yours are like a drop in a pond. They don't matter. What he does care about is money, and if you're not dancing, you're not making money. You won't be able to suck him off to get out of it. The only thing you can do is give him the money you would've made."

"But I don't have any."

"Should've thought of that before you got shit-faced and went out last night instead."

Sapphire gulped down the water. "You're just messing with me, right?"

Michelle shook her head. "I wish I was, honey, but trust me. Just get him the cash and he'll only give you a slap or two."

Sapphire started to cry, and because she was so drunk, it was messy.

Michelle leaned in. "I tell you what, honey—you take off your panties right now, and Roxie's, and I'll give you the money. I'll talk to Jimmy too, get him to go easy on you, since it's your first mistake."

Sapphire blinked at her. "You mean the panties I'm wearing?"

"The very same."

Her face screwed up in disgust. "Are you some sort of perv?"

"Just a businesswoman, honey."

"But then I'll be naked."

"You got a skirt on, don't ya? Just think of yourself as having a secret." When Sapphire failed to move, Michelle got up from the table. "Have it your way. Jimmy'll be in soon. Good luck."

Sapphire let out a little meow like a hurt cat. She reached under the table, and after a few moments of wriggling around, her hand came up holding a pair of lacy blue panties.

Michelle took them from her. "And?"

"What?"

"Roxy's too."

"But she's sleeping."

"Then it'll be easier to get them off her. You can't tell me that girl hasn't had her panties slipped off while she's been asleep before."

"What'll I do when she asks me what happened to them?"

Michelle leaned in, grabbed Sapphire by her ear, and twisted until Sapphire let out a yelp. "You fucking lie. And if you tell anyone about this, I'll make sure Jimmy does a whole lot worse to you than a couple slaps across the face, you feel me, honey?"

Sapphire nodded and disappeared under the table. She came up a few moments later with Roxy's panties.

"Good doing business with you." Michelle reached into her bra and pulled out a hundred dollars—more than what Sapphire would have made that morning. "Go sleep it off and come back tonight. I'll see if Jimmy'll let you dance a night shift."

Sapphire nodded as she took the cash. Michelle gave her a tight smile and shoved the panties in her purse.

"Why?" asked Sapphire, as Michelle walked toward the door.

Michelle turned around, pulled her dick lighter out of her purse, and lit another cigarette. "Always have an exit strategy," she said. She flicked her hair over her shoulder and strolled out the front door.

The club was full that night. Customers were yelling and laughing, pulling bills from wallets and handing them to all the pretty women, who in turn knew they'd be handing most of that money to Jimmy and so were wishing he was dead.

Later, after most of the wallets had left the building, all the pretty girls had gathered in the dressing room to peel off their sweaty costumes for the last time that night. Michelle stood in the corner smoking, deciding if she should leave or if she should try to sneak a pair of panties or two out with her. Before she could decide, she heard a snarl.

"I've had it!" Sara yelled into the full dressing room. All the girls instantly shut up. Sara pointed to Sapphire, who was brushing out her hair. "You fucking cunt, I know it's you."

Sapphire's voice was caught in her throat. Michelle could see her fear. The fact that Sapphire didn't respond only affirmed her own guilt, at least to the other girls. Plus, once Sara had said it, it became true.

Sapphire found her voice. "I'm don't...I..."

"You don't...don't... Speak up, cunt."

Sara began to stalk around the room like a lion tamer, flicking an imaginary whip at Sapphire with every word. "You've been stealing our stuff, you bitch, we all know it's you. Jimmy said to just let it go because of how hard you make the regulars, but fuck it, you took my grandmother's earrings, and enough is enough."

Sapphire should have chosen the name Scarlet—that was the colour she turned as Sara stalked closer and closer. Finally, Sapphire stood up and held her brush out like a bat, like she could stop what was happening. "I didn't steal anything, bitch."

Sara's eyes fired as she leapt at Sapphire. "Oh yeah, let's see about that." She grabbed Sapphire's hair and yanked it. Sapphire screamed. Sara pulled her down to the floor and in a flurry of activity kicked her four times: once in the stomach, once on the arms as they sought to protect her stomach, once in the pussy, and once in the face. Sapphire sobbed into the floor.

"Pull everything out of her cubby. I mean it, everything."

Michelle lit another cigarette. She winced because she knew what they would find, and what they would do, and because she could stop all of this with a few words. Instead, she flicked her dick off and sucked in the smoke.

Two other girls ripped Sapphire's cubicle apart. When they got to the back, they found all the things Michelle had hidden there. They dumped the items on a chair in front of Sara.

Sara pulled Sapphire up by her hair. "Didn't take anything, hey? You stupid fucking bitch, you think we wouldn't notice? I've been buying panties in bulk since mine keep mysteriously disappearing."

At the word *panties*, Sapphire's eyes flicked around the room.

Don't do it, you stupid girl, Michelle willed, don't you fucking do it.

Sapphire opened her mouth.

Michelle strode over and, in one swift motion, punched Sapphire in the face. Sara, taken by surprise, let the unconscious Sapphire fall to the ground.

Michelle shrugged. "Sometimes you just gotta shut a bitch up."

/

Jimmy looked up from his computer at Michelle. "So, I guess she was stealing after all, hey?"

"I guess." Michelle stared back at Jimmy, not giving an inch. He was the sort of man it was better to be strong than fearful around. "Can I smoke in here?"

Jimmy handed her a cigarette from the pack on his desk. "It surprises me she had the balls to do it, you know? She's so innocent. I never thought she'd go up against Sara and the rest of you."

"I guess it's tough to really know a person." Michelle lit the cigarette and pulled in the smoke.

"I have to fire her, you know."

Michelle shrugged.

"It's too bad too, she could've been one of the best."

"Who can tell these days?"

"But maybe I don't have to fire her if she wasn't really the thief. Maybe I could keep her on. It's tough out there for a young girl like her to get a job. Maybe I could give the real thief a warning and some cash to get outta town before the other girls find out. Maybe."

Michelle ran her tongue over her teeth. She knew Jimmy was giving her the opportunity to be the good person she always pretended she was. "With a body like hers, she'll find a new club in a week," she answered.

Michelle stubbed her cigarette in the ashtray and got up to go. Jimmy let her leave without another word, his lips pursed. They had something like respect between them. Maybe it was her age. Maybe it was because she never let him fuck her. But whatever it was, she used it to walk out of the room unscathed one last time.

/

Michelle exhaled into the almost-morning air, knowing she'd never go back inside the club again. Knowing that by the time the sun was fully out and beating down on the town, she'd no longer be a resident. She heard the club door open behind her, followed by the quiet shuffling of feet. Sapphire came to stand beside her, her face puffy and still bleeding.

They stood in silence for a few moments before Sapphire asked one question: "Why?"

Michelle pulled another cigarette out of her purse, flicked the dick lighter. "Because," she said, her lips around a new cigarette, "like I told ya, I always have an exit plan." She handed the dick lighter to Sapphire. "Here, this always brought me good luck." And then she walked away, a swirl of smoke like a crown around her head.

THE DEATH OF HIM CAME TO ME IN MY DREAMS

The small trailer holds our two bodies. Late into the evening, we sip black coffee while picking at stale bannock left by mourners. When Granny speaks, her words crawl out in halting syllables, each break filled with an uncharacteristic silence. We peek at each other in the ring of light cast by the kitchen's sole lamp. Words dribble from her lips. In the wake of death we are unmoored, two strangers in a tin shelter older than two of my lives stacked together.

"He never wanted to go there, you know."

I nod.

"He never had a choice." She glances at me and then out the window. Our reflection a murky shadow against the darkness of the woods. Even the stars refuse to shine on this day of death. "Since before time was created, his ancestors walked there. But he didn't want to."

Her eyes find mine in the glass.

"Every night he would wake up with frost lingering on his skin, mist brought back from the other side."

I knew that cold. But I don't speak. Every morning since you got sick, I wake up gasping, mist wavering above me. A thick layer of frost on the glass panes separates me from the day, mutes the dawn light.

Granny continues. "He never told me much, just bits over the years, but some mornings he would cry into my dressing gown."

"Why didn't he stop?" The words hover between us, and I slip in a tiny lungful of air.

She flicks her eyes to mine. "I don't know, Dawn." I look away from the sorrow in her eyes. Her arthritic fingers, bulging joints that are gripped around her mug of lukewarm tea, tighten. She straightens her back and hauls herself up. "G'night."

She shuffles past me and into the trailer's dark, narrow hallway. Grief pulling her toward a room empty of you—but filled in other ways. Memories. Stuffed in the cracks of the wall. Pushed under the bed. Hidden in the folds of clothing still hanging in the closet. Fragments of thoughts, smells, touches. Tomorrow we will gather your things, the material of your life, and burn it. Send it to where you wait for us now.

People will be back in the morning. Older women in muted colours, murmuring softly as they take over the kitchen, gradually increasing in volume until the house is filled with laughter. Until the floor becomes choked with children, lying on their stomachs to stare up at the TV. Their parents will arrive after work. We will eat—food to heal, to fill spaces. Food that will linger in our bodies for days. And we will burn a portion for you, sending it on spiralling plumes of smoke laced with tobacco, sweetgrass, and sage.

But not until tomorrow. Tonight still belongs to our sadness.

I stumble to the couch and fall back in a whoosh, too numb for a graceful transition from awake to dreams. I lie in the half-formed thoughts of first sleep and I wish you could hear me, that we could still speak like we used to before you closed yourself off from Granny and me.

I knew. Did you know that? I always knew. That you walked in places no one alive is supposed to walk. You murmured between the ticking of the clock in the afternoons as you kept yourself from drifting into naps. You spoke of mist. Of cold. I tried not to listen, but the whole trailer filled with the frozen misty air you would bring back with you in the morning when you left that dream place. When I caught you in the hallway as I was sneaking to the bathroom in that grey morning light, you looked at me with foggy eyes. And I pretended I didn't see what you saw. I pretended we weren't the same. Because you never wanted to talk; you just wanted to forget. So I tried to forget too.

The trailer is too quiet. Even though you hardly spoke in the last few months, you still managed to fill the trailer with your presence, the creaks and scrapes of your movement. And now I don't know what to touch, where to move, without stumbling into the pockets of silence you've left behind.

/

The dream found me, as usual, but this time—the night after your death—it is different. I walk hesitantly down the centre line of the bridge in the near gloom of almost-morning. Plumes of evaporating salt water greet the ever-lightening sky. The bridge is the same as always, shrouded in fog so thick the suspension cables seem to stretch end-lessly into the sky.

The smell is the same too: half-rotting, partly digested fish. Whales and otters swim silently in the murky brown water below. Wind slips itself into the empty spaces in my hair, feeling me. Knowing me.

Then it happens. My heart starts racing, my skin feels like it's burning, my lungs constrict as panic overwhelms me. They say that in extreme moments of fear you either run or you fight. I want to run back to where I came from. But I can't. I can only stand, listen, sense what's coming; the only direction I can move is forward. Farther into the mist. Farther away from the calm light, the peaceful forest.

Swirling in the mist around me are shrouded figures. The echoes of their feet as they shuffle forward send bolts of electricity through me every time one gets too close. The sound of waves crashing into the base of the bridge is rhythmic, deep, and powerful.

Noooooooooo. A cry of anguish from my left.

There you are, beside me. A hunched version of who you were in life. Tears slide from your eyes as you stare into the distance. The pressure around me lifts. I can move freely again. Your presence has unglued me from the march into darkness.

"Grandpa," I whisper.

You try to look at me, I can see the strain around your eyes, but all you can do is move your lips. My girl.

"Grandpa!" I yell.

Your shoulders slump further into your chest. My eyes meet yours—yours are lost, distant. You squint to try to see me.

"This is where you always came? Isn't it?"

You try to pull your eyes from mine, but I won't let you. I'm in control here. As soon as this thought enters my mind, I know it is true. I grab hold of your arm and squeeze.

"Why am I here?" I yell, fighting to be heard over the wind.

You struggle to form words. Dawn, I'm...sorry.

"Why am I here?" I yell again.

The trees on either end of the bridge convulse as the wind batters them; they sway as if they want to uproot and flee. The dark sky is heavy with rain. Black and blues swirl in a threatening mix as the mist around us deepens.

I thought if I didn't teach you...you were a girl. It wasn't supposed to pass on to you. It was supposed to die with me!

My ears rang. "What wasn't supposed to pass to me?"

This curse. Shepherding the dead. Your voice comes from the air all around me.

Your eyes widen and you let out an agonized cry as a silver flash of lightning passes through your hunched body, slicing through your shoulder and zipping back out into the thickening mist. I brace myself for some kind of shared impact, but nothing happens—the bolt was just for you. I scramble to reach out, but you wave me away as you curl into yourself.

I'm okay, you whisper.

A howl echoes behind us. I look back through the haze and see the dark shape of something, an animal maybe, approaching. It's too big to be natural. I shiver, reach out for your hand. It's cold. Too cold. The water thrashes like a churning beast below us, crashing ever higher against the bridge's support beams, whipping itself into frosted waves.

Some of the others on the bridge with us are within an arm's reach, I can hear their inhalations, I know they are there even though I can't see them.

When I look back, your pupils are like pinpricks mirroring the fear and adrenaline coursing through me. For a second you have lifelike strength as you grab my shoulders and pull me toward you.

You must walk the path, Dawn. Your task—you must take me over into the darkness. Take us all. But don't—

Another howl. Whatever creature is behind us is getting closer. Wind whips at my small frame. Freezing rain falls onto my cheeks.

/

I wake with a yelp. Arms outstretched, I reach for you.

Your voice whispers. Take us, one by one, into the darkness. You must. If you don't, you will stay lost, wither—die.

I clutch my head. Was your voice real? My body convulses in fear. I am covered in a sheen of cold sweat. What did you mean?—how would I stay lost? How could I take you—anyone—into darkness? What darkness? My fear of what the darkness might contain is like its own entity. I feel trapped. I can't breathe. I squeeze my eyes shut. I snap the bracelet on my wrist until it hurts, because that pain is real and it calms my fear of what isn't.

❧

I sit in the gloom waiting for Granny to come into the kitchen, to pull out the kettle and boil water for her instant coffee. For the sound of the radio as she tunes the dial from one station to the next, looking for the freshest news. Once those rituals begin, night will officially be over.

Light seeps through the trailer's living room window. My eyes find your faded green armchair by the window, and I see you again as you were in the last months of your life. Staring out at the sky, already almost lifeless, while Granny and I kept the trailer warm with the wood stove you installed years ago. And I realize now that you were willing away the darkness, willing away the mist, the ever-rising stench of salt and fish.

❧

We start with your closet. My hands, Granny's hands, both your sisters' hands. With delicate fingertips we brush over your fragments, the small things you called your own. We don't speak. Maybe because silence is better, or maybe because your presence is still deafening.

Granny holds in her tears for as long as possible before breaking. It starts with a sob. Then a wracking cough. Then a fall onto the bed. A gripping of the blanket that still held your smell, pulled into her face. One of your sisters hauls her up and guides her out of the room.

I fall back into the chair beside your bedroom window. Your clothing is piled around me and I can't imagine not having even one thing you've worn. I start to fold plaid sweaters and worn jeans into piles. Your other sister is slowly making her way through your nightstand, pulling out delicate things: change, an old pin, a book. As your belongings start to pile up, she hands me a bunch of loose papers. I'm about to toss them into a garbage bag when I notice your scrawl. Tilted letters scratched in a stubborn refusal to ever learn cursive.

I unfold the top paper.

The shadow is almost upon me. My time is soon. Good. It will be broken.

I set it aside and read the next one.

Nothing is real. All is the mist. All is the field.

My heart speeds up. What field? The mist I already knew.

My only solace is that it will finally be over. For me. For all of us.

I read through the papers. Each says the same thing. You were looking forward to your death. To your escape from the mist. I think back to my dream. You are still there, in the mist. I hear an echo of your strangled cry in my mind, and the papers fall from my hands and scatter on the floor.

"What is it, Dawn?" Auntie's voice is almost a whisper.

"He's...he's trapped. In the mist. On the bridge."

Her deep brown eyes narrow. She flicks her straight grey hair over one shoulder with fingers covered in silver rings and grabs my arm. She hauls me up, pulls me from your room.

"Auntie, what are you doing?"

She doesn't answer, but pulls me all the way through the back door, skirting the women in the kitchen, the watchful eyes of the kids. She only lets go of my arm when we are a good distance from the trailer. The sky is an overcast blend of cloud and heavy rain yet to fall. The tree branches hold the remains of winter. I shift from my left foot to my right as Auntie lights a cigarette. I squish the dead, blackened leaves.

Auntie looks me up and down as she holds the cigarette up to her mouth, her other hand thrust into her pocket. "What do you know about the mist?"

My face slackens. Could I lie? Did I want to?

"What do you know about the mist?" I ask instead.

She humphs before settling her weight on a bare fallen log. "I see." She takes another drag from her cigarette, pushing the smoke out through her nose. "You know, your grandpa never left this territory. Not once in his life. Did you know that?"

I shake my head no.

"He never even went to the residential school. Nope. He was hidden. By grandfather. They escaped out into the bush. They lived there, just them, until it was safe to go home." She takes a deep breath. "Until we were all different people."

She lets the silence hang, lost in her own memories of that time. Painful and overwhelming, I know from hearing stories.

"He never talked much," I answer.

"I know, he was..." She looks at me, an eyebrow cocked up knowingly, like it used to when I was little and she was telling me to behave without speaking. "He was different."

"How?"

"You know." She pinched her mouth, squinting as she stared at me in challenge. When she gave you that look, you knew you weren't going to win.

I rub my hand over my face, feel the swelling under my eyes from too many tears. I know I must look terrible. As terrible and sad and lonely as everyone else. "I don't know anything," I challenge back.

"You know about the mist, though." She hasn't blinked, has kept her eyes on my face, her mouth pinched.

I give up and look at the ground before collapsing onto the log next to her. I wrap my arms around my knees and feel the tears slipping out as I lean against her steady weight.

"I don't want to go back there," I whisper. "It killed him."

"No, Dawn. It is death."

"What?"

"I wasn't supposed to know. But I was jealous. Your grandfather was always given different food, given special jobs, given story after story, song after song. He knew the names of things, the real names of things, and he talked to these things." She shakes her head and takes a long inhale. "The rest of us were just normal, I guess. But I snuck where I wasn't supposed to sneak. And from our grandfather's lips, I heard about the mist." She drops the cigarette to the damp ground and grinds it into the mud with her toe. "It's not something to be fearful of."

She reaches out and strokes my head. "Your job, the thing you are responsible for now, is to lead."

"Lead who?"

"The dead." She grabs my chin as she says this, looks deep into my eyes. She doesn't cry. But she feels. I close my eyes against her sadness.

I can see the bridge. I can see the way the mist curls around the tops of the trees. I can hear the scurrying of animals in the distant forest. I can sense the ghosts as they shuffle aimlessly in the darkness. They are lost without a guide through the mist.

✦

My throat feels scratchy. The long days with black-clothed grievers has taken a toll on me. My hands are dry, the moisture sucked out from others' hands brushing over mine. Neighbours grip my fingers, let me feel their sorrow at your passing. Dishes need to be washed in the sink after everyone leaves for the night. Granny is too tired at the end of the day to do anything but collapse on the couch in front of the TV.

I want them to go away. To never come back. I want to be alone. I want to sleep. Curl up in my bed. Close my eyes. Let the darkness come for me. I want to be in the dream because I need to see you.

I let my clothing slide into a pile on the floor. Settle between the heavy comforter and sigh into its warmth and safety. I want to believe that someday my dreams will go back to ordinary, back to how they were before you got sick. But I know they never will.

/

The wind howls. The trees bow against it. Waves rise and I can feel the cold sting of the ocean against my face. Rain falls from the purple sky and lightning cuts the mist, revealing the contorted faces of the dead. My screams are drowned out by their cries. Then you are beside me, your fingers pressing into my wrist.

Guide me. Your voice louder than everything else. I don't know this place anymore. You must.

The bridge rocks with the force of the storm. I look ahead at the howling darkness. I don't want to go there. Only death lurks there. I know that now. I can feel it.

Guide me. You shake me as you plead.

The moans of the others on the bridge fill me with terror. Their hands claw at me, desperate in the face of the storm. I try to back away. Run back into the forest. But my feet are locked forward. I've lost control over the dream.

Your face distorts in pain as silver flashes pierce your skin. You let me go as your body spasms. My heartbeat skips erratically. I try to run to the edge of the bridge—I want to leap into the waters, because anything would be better than this, but I still can't move.

There is a bear-like growl, and something is coming toward me—toward us. I look down at you writhing in pain as you beg me to help.

I want to wake up. This dream, this bridge, everything here is real, as real as my waking life. You grip the hem of my pants and my heart stalls. I cough deeply, and it starts to beat again frantically. You don't deserve this. I can't hear you—the wind is stealing your words from my ears—but I can see your mouth forming them as you plead with me. Your eyes, they are hollow, but they bore into mine until I see it, a flicker of hope—your hope in me. Your fingers let go as another bolt of silver passes through you. You convulse. In a panic, my own arms trembling as much as yours, I reach down and grip your shoulder. You stop shivering. I look ahead. The heart of the storm in front of us. The growling from the woods behind us grows louder. I crouch beside you. Pull your body against mine.

Please. Your voice is almost gone, but my whole body hears it. Lead me.

"How?"

Just walk.

I grip you under the armpits, haul you up, drag your weight forward. The more we walk, the more you're able to hold yourself up. My feet know the way, even if I don't. They lead me through the outstretched hands of the other ghosts.

The closer we move to the middle of the bridge and the closer to the darkness of the storm we get, the fainter the moans from the ghosts become. Into the heart of the howling wind and rain and forked lightning—we march across the bridge, bowing our heads against the force of the gale. I keep count of my heartbeats, one after another. We begin to pull through to the other side. At the far end of the bridge, the trees stand straighter. The wind calms. But the mist still swirls around us. I stare into the maw of the dark forest and my stomach cramps. I don't want to go any closer. Like a rabbit trembling as it's exposed on the top of a hill, I feel open to that darkness.

Thank you, you say as you slide away from me. You stand at the edge of the forest and take a few deep breaths. It won't be long.

"Grandpa." I hear the tremble of panic in my voice.

Don't you see? You point ahead.

And then I do see. Beyond the darkness is a pinprick of light. When I train my eyes on it, my body stops shaking. My trembling evaporates.

"Am I dead?" I ask. "Why am I here?"

You're not dead. This is your job—your curse and your gift. I thought that because I didn't have a grandson, all of this would disappear. I never imagined you would inherit this. I'm sorry. I should have taught you. I should have...

"Is this why you never left our territory?"

Yes.

My stomach flutters as a realization hits me: I'll never leave either.

I try to absorb this. I'll be tied to our land forever. Possibilities of a life in the city, of travelling the world, of anything new—gone. Just like that. My eyes fill with tears and my throat constricts.

The path I guided was a field. It's different for each of us. My grandfather followed a path across a frozen lake. His grandfather, a beach. You, a bridge.

I pull my eyes from the distant light. It is worth it to look into your eyes one more time. You look different. Lighter. Your shoulders are straight like in the photograph I love, the one in the living room from when you and Granny are young. Your face is the one I've always known, kind and thoughtful, but unlined now.

You pull me into a tight hug, then release me. Go, my girl. You can't stay for this part. Not until it's your turn to be led.

"What do you mean?"

As I was dying, the path became fainter. Then I found myself on your bridge. One day you'll find yourself on someone else's path. Maybe your grandchild's. Hopefully you'll teach them to walk before the time comes. Not like me. I'm sorry for abandoning you, my girl. But I know you can do this.

The wind pushes me away from you, back onto the bridge, back into the mist. After one last squeeze of your hand, I let myself be propelled, my silent goodbye wishing you well as you step forward into the light.

❧

People here speak of you fondly. They come by with fish or moose, or for a chat. But nothing we do fills your space in the trailer.

The bridge won't let me leave, I know that now. I am glued to this land. Like you, and your grandfather—all the grandfathers. But it's okay. The mist rises off me when I wake, and I go on.

I clean. I cook. I take care of Granny.

She is closing her eyes beside me now. Her chin is tapping at her chest, but she doesn't want to go to bed. The bed you shared. So I offer her an arm and lead her to the couch instead. It dwarfs her tiny frame as she sinks into the cushions that smell like the lavender candles I burned all day. I pile blankets on her and leave the room with the TV buzzing, because you always spoke to her as she drifted off, guiding her to sleep—a quiet voice to let her know she's not alone.

TAKING SPACE

All the clamouring voices who want their place in this book.

All these voices pouring out in a rush at the end of this story, pleading for me to include their tales, or their rantings, or the love letters written fourteen years ago to someone they still yearn for.

All these voices interrupt my afternoon naps, will themselves to the forefront of my mind. Spill their decrepit secrets into my ears until I can't stand it anymore.

All their clamouring voices drive me insane.

All their clamouring voices pull me under.

All their clamouring voices desecrate my soul with the filth they carry that transfers to me with every word I write.

All their clamouring voices fill me to empty.

I scream shut up shut up shut up—fine.

All their clamouring voices, written at last, as the final letter stamps the page.

But why do I hear them still? All these clamouring voices.

ACKNOWLEDGEMENTS

I would like to send a big thank-you to all the wonderful people who over the years had a hand in editing these stories; you all made them better. This book took a long time to come together, with stories coming into my life at just the right times. They deal with so many different movements through my life, and embedded in these pages are so many memories, I can't even count. Thank you to all the people who have embarrassing, confessional, and deeply personal conversations in public where writers can eavesdrop and jot your perfect one-liners down. I wrote these stories in Vancouver, BC, and I feel the beautiful grey skies that are emblematic of that incredible coast have made their way into these pages, and so I guess I would like to acknowledge the rain, and the serenity that it provides.

Thank you to my wonderful readers. Those who read draft after draft, you know who you are. And thank you to those of you who picked this book off the shelf and have now read it.

Thank you to the following publications, in which earlier versions of these stories appeared: *Bawaajigan: Stories of Power, Best Canadian Short Stories 2021, The Malahat Review, The Quilliad, The Humber Literary Review, Joyland, Litro, InShades Magazine, The Puritan, Grain Magazine*, and *Exile Magazine*.

And finally, thanks to a very special cat friend named Patches, who would be devastated if she didn't get her own thank-you.

INVISIBLE PUBLISHING produces fine Canadian literature for those who enjoy such things. As an independent, not-for-profit publisher, our work includes building communities that sustain and encourage engaging, literary, and current writing.

Invisible Publishing has been in operation for over a decade. We released our first fiction titles in the spring of 2007, and our catalogue has come to include works of graphic fiction and nonfiction, pop culture biographies, experimental poetry, and prose.

We are committed to publishing diverse voices and experiences. In acknowledging historical and systemic barriers, and the limits of our existing catalogue, we strongly encourage writers from LGBTQ2SIA+ communities, Indigenous writers, and writers of colour to submit their work.

Invisible Publishing is also home to the Bibliophonic series of music books and the Throwback series of CanLit reissues.

If you'd like to know more, please get in touch: info@invisiblepublishing.com